HIGHWAY ONE, ANTARCTICA

Justin Herrmann

MadHat Press
Asheville, North Carolina

MadHat Press
MadHat Incorporated
PO Box 8364, Asheville, NC 28814

The Library of Congress has assigned
this edition a Control Number of
2014930599

ISBN 978-0-9885490-7-4 (paperback)

Text by Justin Herrmann
Cover art by Marc Vincenz
Book and cover design by MadHat Press

www.madhat-press.com

for Mae and Winter

CONTENTS

DOREEN AND THE PIG

I had a girlfriend named Doreen who had a liver like a heavy bag. Hell with drinking me under the table, she could drink me out of the house, into and back out of the woods, and the eighteen miles down 51 North to the ER if she wanted.

She lived in a one-bedroom single-wide with her parents up in the hills south of Carbondale. Her dad grew tomatoes and raised a few chickens. He was a small man with thick hands I would grow to envision strangling me. They had a pig named Wally. A pig as big as a fridge and about as mobile.

Doreen took me to see this pig. They had a trashcan full of beer near the pen. She said, "The Hamm's isn't meant for irony. It's the cheapest they got at the gas station." She picked up one of the Hamm's and leaned over and held it out to him. Gentle as a nurse. He pierced the can with his teeth and swallowed the beer as it foamed into his mouth, then he chomped the can a couple times and spat it out.

"Jesus, where'd he learn to do that?" I said.

"One for him, one for me," she said, and cracked open a warm Hamm's and handed one to me.

One beer after another. I don't know how many, but I was in college at the time and it was more than I ever drank in one night in the dorms. At one point Doreen lit a cigarette. I thought she'd have a way of giving Wally one too, but instead she just took a few drags and said, "A minute ago even my bones wanted this smoke. Funny how that works." She had a way of talking like that. Saying things I couldn't respond to.

I stayed the weekend. One for Wally, one for Doreen, one for me. At one point her dad refilled the trashcan of Hamm's. Then it was one for him too.

After the semester ended that spring, I didn't re-enroll. I set up a tent near Doreen's trailer and stayed for a time. I'd split wood. Doreen's mother taught me to hunt mushrooms. Sometimes I'd hunt mushrooms while everyone else slept, then I'd drink beer with Wally. One for me and one for him.

There's other things I could tell you about. Those eighteen miles to the ER, or about prying one of Doreen's dad's canines from between my third and fourth knuckles with a Buck knife. There's more I could say, but all I care to tell you now is about Doreen and that pig. I've been with more attractive women, but I've never been more attracted to a woman.

I never saw anyone touch Wally. Just reach out and hand him beer. He barely spilled a drop.

POLAR PLUNGE

Down here on the coast of Antarctica, the fish are almost as strange as the women. When I pull the spotty greenish-gray creature up through the hole in the ice, two things cross my mind: I wonder if I have enough time to get back to Station and call Julie who is thousands of miles away in Illinois and will soon be waiting to hear from me, and I wonder if the girl that brought me out to this fish hut will continue taking off clothes.

"Should I feel guilt about it?" she says, and unhooks one of the straps of her Carhartt coveralls. "That this fish is going to slowly be cooked alive, dead by the time the water reaches 38 degrees?" She's an assistant to a team of biologists and she tells me all about it, that they will remove his liver, chop it into tiny pieces, turn it into a slurry, and then separate it into individual cells. Something having to do with cellular trauma research. An end like that makes you think.

I pick my fishing pole and beer up off the floor of the hut, and set the pole upright in a corner and gauge that the beer is still half full. I take a big drink, and look over at her. Not because she's beautiful. She's not. I don't mean she's a goat, but the collar of her t-shirt is stretched out and hangs low over her unstrapped shoulder, and her skin is freckled and dull and looks like it's made out of construction paper, like I could jam a finger right through. It's not at all like the slick skin, moisturized nightly with virgin coconut oil, I've grown used to. Still, there is something about her, an allure, something unexplainable like the appeal of professional wrestling. I take another big drink. Try not to think more about ends.

I'd been noticing the fish girl around Station for weeks. I'd see her in the early morning hours at the lab, dumping coolers of live fish into seawater tanks in the aquarium, or sometimes she'd be tucked away in a corner doing headstands. I had never been much into fishing, had never much understood the appeal until a few years ago when I worked up in northwestern Alaska and some of the locals took me ice fishing with them a couple times. They'd haul twenty-pound sheefish through their holes with heavy line tied to pieces of scrap wood. Women would gut and fillet the fish right on the ice before they froze. I wondered how a science operation here on the other side of the planet compared. I wondered how this girl caught her fish. I wondered if she'd let me come with her.

Mostly I'd see the fish girl at the bar, always alone. My boss, who is known around here as Donald Duck, always both names, and who I have drinks with most days after work noticed me noticing her too.

"Hombre," he told me. "You've been away from home way too long." I knew what he meant by that. He's seen a picture of my girlfriend, Julie. "Who the fuck is Helen of Troy?" he said when I first showed him. Big green and gold eyes like a giant cat, a full set of lips so confident and content they belong on a corpse. She is the most beautiful girl I'll ever be with. I'd consider myself more lucky if I thought I could keep her.

12

Me and Donald Duck work together here at McMurdo Station in Antarctica, the metropolis and gateway of the continent, a noisy, filthy place full of firefighters and electricians, cargo handlers and HR specialists, van drivers and network administrators, pilots and bakers, labor allocation specialists, all brought here to the bottom of the world so science can be conducted in a comfortable setting; we're packed together so tightly I haven't taken a crap by myself since I've been here. Me and Donald Duck fit in as the night janitorial staff, a job he's been doing for the past eight austral summer seasons, August till February. A job he'll be doing till global warming melts this continent clean out from under his broom. And with as much turnover as there is across the board here, he's been able to carve out a nice little gig for himself, and by association, me. By the time we finish stripping and waxing all the floors on Station, tourists will be trolling for marlins from the back of yachts in these waters.

Early this morning, around 8:00, Me and Donald Duck rinsed the volcanic filth from our extractors after a night of cleaning endless amounts of grit from the Comms Shop carpets, and headed for the bar. The fish girl was already there and we took our place a couple stools down from her. She had a bag of American Spirit tobacco open on the bar top and was making a pile of roll-your-owns between glasses of Black Velvet.

I laid a five down for a round of Coronas and tried to imagine what Julie would lower herself to order here. "She put me on hold," I told Donald Duck. "I call, same time I do every week, in the middle of my sleep schedule for her convenience, and she clicks over to the incoming-call line."

"My first wife," Donald Duck said. "I don't think I could describe her face to a sketch artist if I had to."

The bartender who works full-time as a mechanic here at McMurdo served us our bottles with grease-stained hands and chipped nails. I drank from the beer. Then I put it down and picked up my hook and yarn.

"It's all about tension," Donald Duck said. "Just let your hands find their rhythm."

I made it a goal to cut back on my drinking while I was at McMurdo, but I was doing better at my other goal, which was to learn anything that counted as an art or craft and would make me look well-rounded like Julie's friend Chad, a guy who dabbles in fashion design. But I've met Chad. Seems to me his talent consists of abusing low-cost drugs and shopping at thrift stores.

So far I've only crocheted two lopsided pot holders. When Donald Duck offered to teach me to crochet, he said I'd drink less because my hands would be occupied. But most mornings we're either at the bar, or in his room drinking the two six packs we're allotted to buy from the station store.

"When she clicked back over," I said, "she told me Chad had a crisis on his hands and needed her to come model. Told me to call back today if I wanted." If I wanted. "Julie," I had told her, "I'll call, please be waiting."

The fish girl unzipped a fanny pack, placed her pile of cigarettes in it, and zipped it back up. She had a head full of wiry black braids tied off at the ends with colored rubber bands. Her face was as colorful as a Christmas ornament, with a tattoo of a spider web, no joke, inside the folds of her ear, and silver rings looped through her eyebrows. There was a red patch, a rash of some sort, near her mouth. I have a beautiful girlfriend now, but I've kissed mouths like that.

The lines of my third potholder were already starting to go diagonal. You can't have a hobby like fishing or rock climbing here. Anything that might interfere with nature is reserved solely for the grantees who conduct science. For guys like me or Donald Duck, the only chance we have to see much more than the inside of toilet bowls is if one of the grantees takes us somewhere with them. When I fished with the locals in Alaska, an entire four-person family would pile onto one Honda 4-wheeler with their homemade poles and nets, thermoses of coffee and bags of Fritos and drive out onto the frozen Chukchi Sea or Noatak River for an afternoon. They'd stick fish heads on hooks, or sometimes drop the hooks in with nothing on them. I wondered what the fish girl used for bait as I watched her tilt the glass and drain the rest of her Black Velvet while the ice rattled off her teeth.

The fish girl stood up from her stool and walked towards the door. I shifted a little in my stool, and then I set down my hook and yarn and walked over to her while she was putting on her parka.

"We haven't met," I said to her, and reached out and shook her hand and introduced myself.

"The name's Tia," she said. Her hand felt like it didn't have any bones in it.

It was hard to hear her over ZZ Top roaring from speakers overhead, even though the bar was nearly empty during these early hours, so I shouted, "My partner and I, we wondered if you wanted to have a drink with us?"

She looked as if I'd just asked her to walk on hot coals. "I have to get back to work," she said. But then she added, "I can have a quick one."

That's a big difference between contractors like me and Donald Duck, and grantees. Us contractors will lose our jobs over everything. Donald Duck told me four hundred people apply every year to scrub toilets. We're not hard to replace. And people here are constantly aware of the threat of being replaced. Zero alcohol on the job, zero contact ever with wildlife, unless under the clear supervision of a grantee. Earlier this year someone got fired for throwing a rock at a skua that ripped a sandwich from his hand.

I walked back to the bar and she followed with her parka still on. "Three BVs and ice," She said to the bartender. She pointed her index finger gun-fashion at me and said, "They'll be on this guy."

I laid a five and three ones for the drinks and tip on the bar. I planned to make small talk with her, buy a couple more rounds, get the nerve to ask her if she ever brings anyone out fishing with her.

But she didn't waste any time even for introductions with Donald Duck, or to cheers when the drinks were poured. She picked up her glass and drank her Black Velvet without even a nod of appreciation. Then she put her glass down and looked at our yarn and crochet hooks and said, "If you boys are interested in giving a different sort of hooking a try, meet me in about fifteen outside Crary, Phase III."

Donald Duck was crocheting away on another scarf he'll sell to some other first-timer here, someone who wants to send something authentic Antarctic to a loved one. Without looking away from the scarf he said, "Well, sweetheart, you look just like my first wife, so I'd have to charge you double."

She took one of her cigarettes out. "Your offer's been noted. If you're not there, I'm not going to wait." She stood up and pushed her stool against the bar, brought the cigarette to that mouth and walked out.

Donald Duck has told me he owes me. He got his name because he used to go into the sauna with a shirt but no towel or anything else covering his bottom half. The saunas are unisex and he's been banned from using them. Sometimes during our shift I'll put up CLOSED signs on one, and stand outside it as if I am about to clean, while Donald Duck sits bare-assed inside. It's some kind of spiritual need for him or something. I don't understand it.

"Hombre," he said, "opportunities like this don't come up much for guys like you and me. Come in tonight a few hours late if you need. Just don't let Medusa turn you to stone."

I walked down to the Crary lab and Tia was loading equipment or something into the back of a PistenBully, a boxy tracked vehicle. Having just been at the bar, I wondered if I'd be allowed to take a leak out on the ice, or if I should ask her if I should grab a pee bottle. But then she climbed down and saw me and said, "Just me and you?" and I nodded and didn't ask about the bottle.

I wasn't sure where or how far we were going, but we didn't go anywhere more than ten miles an hour. The PistenBully was as loud as a lawnmower. I saw Tia's mouth move a few times, but I couldn't make out a word over the engine, so I looked out the window. We drove through town, past the backside of the dorms, past stacks of orange USAP MILVANS, giant fuel containers, and the incinerator building that was built years ago but never used for that purpose, just another storage warehouse now. We drove past the pier made out of layers of cable and ice, used for the annual vessel offload. We headed out onto the sea ice just past a wooden hut originally designed to be used in the Australian Outback that was instead used right here by Robert Falcon Scott a hundred years ago, one that still holds his leftover boxes of cocoa and biscuits. Not much leaves this place except people.

I've up and left women before. Sometimes I'd leave in the middle of an argument, or even just a conversation, and go drive around. Other times I'd go on a bender for days. One time

I traded up for a blonde with a pair of legs that would make an antelope horny. Things have been different since I've been with Julie. If she says the ocean is red, I say as red as a cardinal. She's a sensitive girl. She cries in her sleep and wakes me up constantly. Before I left I bought her a giant stuffed penguin, but I know that is no substitute for the warmth of another body.

Out on the sea ice there was a single orange and blue wooden building about as big as a king-size bed. Tia pulled up near the building and cut the engine. "Fish hut zero three," she said. We hadn't gone far. Close enough that we could have waved to the ghosts of Scott and his crew had they been watching us from the porch of their hut. We got out and Tia unlocked the fish hut. There were no smells out in the open air on the ice. At McMurdo, things smell like diesel, or grease, or men. Even the women smell like men.

"There's a couple coolers in the back of the Bully. Grab them," she said.

I pulled the coolers out. They were the kind of round yellow coolers you find filled with lemonade at company picnics. The one was empty and had some kind of tube and disk cut and taped into the lid, an aerator for the fish. With the locals I fished with in Alaska, there was never a reason to keep anything alive after they caught it. The other cooler was heavy with something *wushing* around inside it.

It was a bright and still day. I had seen the temperature that morning, but the warmth of twenty-two degrees in the Antarctic makes me realize how little I understand about the world. There was a window in each side of the hut, and a section of the floor was cut out over a hole through the ice big enough for a small bear to jump through. A flimsy plastic tube about the width of my head hung from the ceiling to a few inches over the hole. Wires were rigged from it along a beam on the ceiling to a gas generator, and warm air blew straight down from the tube keeping the hole from freezing back up.

"Here you go, princess," Tia said, "you get Barbie. Anakin Skywalker is always mine." She handed me a tiny pink rod that had a picture of Barbie's face on the reel. I pushed a button on the handle and lights on the reel started blinking. She reached into her coat pocket and then handed me a small glittery jig that matched my rod.

It was cozy enough that we set our rods down and took off our standard-issue down parkas. She had on a dirty hoodie and Carhartt coveralls. Looked like she could be fishing at a pond in Minnesota. We tied the jigs to our lines and she took the lid off the heavy cooler and pulled out a can of Tui and handed it to me. Then she pulled out one for herself.

"Fishing and beer," she said, "like cookies and milk." She picked up her rod and stepped near the hole. She took a big drink of beer and dropped her line into the water.

I looked down into the hole. A few feet of turquoise ice glowed beneath the surface. I had never seen ice that looked like that, and I wanted to kneel down and taste it. But instead I dropped my line in too.

"You want it to go about twenty-five feet," she said. "Close to the bottom. They are slow, sluggish things. Won't bite unless you drop it right in front of their face or they run into it." I was surprised by the pull of the current. Everything was so static on the surface. No wind blowing for once, not a cloud in the sky. I looked out the window across the miles of frozen ocean that connects Ross Island, where McMurdo sits, to the actual Antarctic continent, fenced in by a group of mountains called the Royal Society Range.

"Give it a jig every few seconds," she said. "You'll barely feel him take, but when you do, act quick. Give him a hell of a tug." She was like a machine: right hand jig, left hand bring the beer to her mouth. She finished the beer, crumpled the can, and tossed it in a corner behind me. Then she took one of her cigarettes out of her fanny pack and smoked that.

I couldn't think of anything good to say, so I said, "The fish. Can you eat them?"

"About as edible as Legos," she said. "Never tried either, though." Every time she'd take a drag of her cigarette she turned her head so that that rash was looking right at me. So I looked back at it. But even Julie, when it comes down to it, isn't perfect. The way she eats, for one thing. Sounds like a wet-dry vac.

"So how did you get into this stuff—fish research?" I said.

"Oh, no," she said. "I'm no scientist or anything. I just catch the fish. Pretty mindless work. Sometimes after sitting here all day, I find myself surprised I have a cooler full of fish."

I knew what she meant about the mindless work. It was the reason I've been a janitor so long. Donald Duck tells me the work is art, which is why he says he does it. He'll spend a whole ten-hour shift stripping one lab. Get down on his knees and scrape every imperfection off the floor with a straight razor. He's told me he's going to start his own floor-care business someday. I don't have the heart to tell him he'd never make a dime the way he works.

"How about you?" she said. "Why'd you come here?"

I swallowed the rest of my beer and set the empty can down next to hers. "I guess because I didn't think I could," I said.

Early on with Julie, she lived near a college and about a dozen bars. She had an upstairs apartment with a nice balcony. Most nights we'd stand out there, talk about the sort of things we talked about back then. Diet Pepsi, owls, the Bermuda Triangle. When the bars let out at two a.m., people would rumble by below, yelling, searching. Once in a while some guy would look up at us, his face flashing red from the glow of the neon Budweiser sign across the road, and say something like *Julie, is that you? Long time no see. Call me sometime.* I was getting old enough to know we all had histories. Mine included saying things to women I'd be embarrassed to admit, things I knew I'd never say to Julie, so those guys calling up to her didn't bother me much back then. These days our apartment is four stories up and overlooks a parking lot for a daycare center, but still, what would she say back if someone yelled up to her now?

Tia and me were at it for a while. Drinking and jigging. The plastic rod felt light in my hand. Weighed less than any shoe in Julie's wardrobe. At one point Tia stopped jigging, reeled in her line. She took off her hoodie, tossed it in one of the corners of the hut. She had on just a thin t-shirt under her coveralls, one transparent enough that I could make out the polka-dotted pattern on her bra through it, and then she knelt down facing the wall of a different corner and balanced herself onto her forearms and extended into a headstand. We talked with her upside down like that. She told me more about the fish. About the anti-freeze in their blood. I talked about carpet cleaning for some reason. The aggressive brightness of the sky stayed the same out the window the whole time. It would stay the same even when it got late.

I was thinking maybe the current was too strong for me to feel anything. Maybe I had been feeling nibbles after all and wasn't reacting. But Tia hadn't had any luck either. So I kept at it. There was no reason not to. It felt good being out there with the anticipation that something could bite at any moment. Or nothing might bite, but I liked knowing there was an element to it that was out of my control.

After a while Tia let her feet swing back down to the floor, one heavy rubber bunny boot, then the other. She sat down and unlaced those boots and pulled them off. She rolled the heavy, gray, government-issued wool socks off her feet, and a smell like Cool Ranch Doritos filled the fish hut. I could see greenish-blue veins through the skin of her feet. She reached down and cracked the knuckles on her toes one foot at a time. Then she stood up and walked to the ice hole. She sat down at the very edge of the hole and put her foot into the water. "Funny how it works," she said. "How just dipping a single toe in will send a shudder through your entire body." She drew her foot back out of the water, but stayed sitting near the edge. "With the salt content, this water is actually below freezing. About thirty degrees."

"Just seeing you dip a toe in is enough to make me shudder," I said.

I felt another nibble I wasn't sure was a nibble, and thought, what the hell, and gave the rod a good pull. I felt a bit of a pull back and the tip of the rod bent.

"You got one. Reel it in," she said, and stood up and stood back from the hole.

There was barely any fight in the fish. She was about five inches long. All eyes and head that tapered off into a puny body. You couldn't scrape off enough filet for a piece of sushi.

"It's a Bernie. *Trematomus bernacchii*. Not much of one, but they're all keepers in these waters." She took the fish in her hand and unhooked it. I set my rod on the floor and took the lid off the cooler with the aerator while she held the fish. I got down on my stomach over the hole and plunged the cooler in and felt the bite of the water rush over my hands and lifted it out half full. She dipped her hand into the cooler and released her grip on the Bernie.

The fish hunkered completely motionless on the bottom of the cooler. She screwed the lid back on. Turned on the aerator. Neither of us picked back up our poles, and neither of us said anything again for a while. Then she said the thing about guilt and the fish's liver getting chopped up, and unhooked the strap of her Carhartt's.

As she unhooks the other strap of her coveralls, I take a drink of beer and look at the floor. There's little pebbles and volcanic grit all over. Little bits tracked in from the bottoms of boots each day. It makes me wish I had a broom and dustpan. I take another drink of beer and say, "It's not what I expected," meaning Antarctica.

I don't know what she thinks I mean by it, but then she balls up the bottom hem of her shirt into her fists and says, "I know what you mean. Let's polar plunge." She pulls her shirt over her head and her armpits are so hairy it looks like she has a raccoon in a headlock. Julie goes to a salon regularly to get waxed. Not a stray hair anywhere on her body.

I finish the rest of the can of beer and watch her slip her coveralls off. She has a rash on her chest and the insides of her thighs the color of the rash near her mouth. Then I start undressing too. This is crazy. We have no towels for one thing. For another, how hard is it to climb out of an ice hole?

I see Tia looking at me, watching me undress. Looking at the tattoo on my ribs, one that I got matching with a girlfriend when I was nineteen, a girlfriend who wouldn't look at me the last time I ran into her, a girlfriend I nonetheless believed when she told me she loved me. "It's supposed to be Johnny Cash, but it looks more like Kim Jong Il," I say.

"It's just an in-and-out-type thing," she says as she unhooks her bra. "Don't go too far under."

23

Justin Herrmann

I take off my watch and note the time. Julie will be home from work any minute and then will wait by the phone. Over the weak gurgle of the aerator, I can hear Tia start taking deeper breaths. The Cool-Ranch-Dorito smell still hangs in the air strong enough to taste. The fishing poles, the jigs, the empty beer cans, everything gleams in the sunlight. There might be dozens of shiftless Bernies in the darkness right below our feet. My socks are two different colors; one of them is yellow with mesh vents for running, it's from a pair Julie gave me last year for my birthday. I take that one off last while I wait for Tia to make the next move.

CRAYON WAY OUTSIDE THE LINES

This guy I know, Cotton, used to be my stepdad but he's not anymore, he coughs up blood and pisses himself. He's going to die soon. Doctors told him so. He's a drunk. I paid him a visit today. Seemed like the right thing to do. This guy he lives with, another drunk, a hide-the-whiskey-in-the-grill-so-the-wife-and-kids-don't-know-I'm-drinking kind of drunk, kept telling me how soon Cotton was going to die. "Son of a bitch won't make it till Christmas," he'd say, "just want you to know the truth," and he'd be sure to look me right in the eye, because we're both men, and give me that kind of stern nod so I know he's not just telling me some shit, so I know Cotton is really at the end, so I can see evidence up close for myself that a life of drinking really will make you die young. So I thanked the guy for telling me that, and he must think I appreciated his no-bullshit approach, but I think I thanked him because what else could I say?

I had a dog that got ran over once, a beagle-lab mix, the first pet that was actually mine. An old man ran him over. Guy looked about eighty or so, maybe shouldn't have been driving. I was getting a handjob from a girl who would never be my girlfriend because I thought she was too fat when the guy brought my dead dog to my door. It was uncomfortable. I was sad. I thanked him for bringing my dog back.

Cotton, this other drunk, and I sat around a table littered with children's schoolwork, old newspapers, and empty cigarette packs. Cotton and I drank from Budweiser tallboys. His buddy drank from a pint of Old Crow. There was a coloring book opened to a picture of Jesus holding a loaf of bread in one hand and a fish in the other. Jesus was smiling. It was colored poorly. Crayon way outside the lines.

"You want to go grab something to eat. It'll be on me," I said to Cotton.

"I haven't had much of an appetite. I can throw in some fries if you're hungry," he said. His speech was slow and mellow. He didn't want to leave the comfort of his tallboy. His face looked leathery and well-worn, like the cover of an old dictionary. There were small red bumps on the cheek below one of his eyes.

The air was stale and musty, but with a mild sweetness, maybe from an insufficient air-freshener, or maybe from bowls of unfinished children's cereal that lined the cracked linoleum on the kitchen counter. Dried ramen noodles clung to the carpet and to a one-eyed, pink stuffed toad that lay on the floor near my feet. The place reminded me of my neighborhood when I was a kid. Small boxy houses with chipped paint and overgrown lawns. Someone with purple and lime-green shutters. Cracked sidewalks. An old Chevy on cinderblocks in a front yard that will never be fixed.

I remembered those mornings before school, feeding myself, my mother already long at work. The Estrada family, whose boys would steal my free-lunch vouchers on the way to school, lived in a house down the street with a chain-link-fenced-in front yard. I remember hearing Emory, the youngest Estrada boy, got stabbed in the heart in prison a couple years back. Shook his girlfriend's baby to death. He and I ran around a bit together in high school. We pissed in all the drinking fountains in the school once after a Saturday detention. He said he liked to piss on girls after sex. I didn't doubt it. He was one of those guys I never felt quite comfortable around but considered a friend anyway.

I watched as Cotton's hands trembled as he struggled to light a match for a cigarette. I don't remember him ever having been a smoker before. His eyes looked up and met mine as he raised the match to his cigarette.

"You smoke?" he said.

"No," I said.

I picked up a newspaper from the table and stared at the lines, pretending to read it, or maybe I really tried to read it and just couldn't focus on the words. I searched for something to say, but nothing felt right. I mean, it's not like there wasn't stuff I could have talked about. Jobs I've had. Ex-girlfriends. My current girlfriend whose arms are proportionately too fat and who has an eye that droops a bit, but isn't bad-looking otherwise, and who can make one hell of a coconut cream pie. And it's not like I don't remember things Cotton and I did together, or things he said. It's not like I didn't have shit to say, but where do you start after all those years? I would've liked to have remembered good advice he may have given me, or remembered instances where he and I did something together, like building sandcastles or something, something I could tell him about and make him feel good. But I didn't think of anything, not like that.

Someone told me, a former boss who also happens to be a drunk but who has had some luck in business and who doesn't have any kids so he's not looked at as being a deadbeat like other drunks, he told me that you can't die gracefully if you don't live gracefully. I don't buy it. Does anyone ever really die gracefully? Does anyone ever really live gracefully?

27

I wondered what kinds of things Cotton knows about his daughter, my sister. Did he know about her near-fatal drug overdose? How she was out at the lake banging morphine with two older guys, and got dropped off unconscious and topless in front of the emergency room? And did he share my humiliation, hearing stories about how she sucked off Lester Langtree behind the dumpster of the old theater for a burger-fry combo; wondering if people are laughing about her when they walk by whispering to each other; dealing with people coming up and saying "Dude, did you hear about how your..." and you can only cut them off saying you don't care? But of course you care, how can you not, she's your family, and you remember things about her like when you and her used to spend hours finding flat stones and trying to skip them down the creek and how she sat silent on the muddy creek bank with you while you wept like a baby after Ryan Estrada cracked you in the ear with a muddy, rusted size D battery and she never mentioned a word about it to anyone. You want to hug her and shake her and beg her to stop fucking up, but how can you when you are aware you are a piece of shit yourself?

Cotton put out his cigarette in an ashtray the shape of a moose. At one time it may have been a cookie cutter. He drank the last of his tallboy and crushed the sides in before laying it back on the table.

"There's more beer in the fridge. Grab one for you and one for me," he said. "Doctor says I shouldn't drink anymore, but I have a couple a day."

"That's not bad," I said.

His friend drank from his whiskey. "Son of a bitch is becoming a regular Mother-Fucking-Theresa," he said.

My girlfriend tells me I drink too much. She's probably right. We've been fighting a lot lately, her and me. One minute she says we can't go on like this. The next she says she can't go on without me. Really the fights are over nothing. Take this one morning a couple weeks back. We're in bed drinking Heaven Hill and tonic. Maybe she's kissing on my neck a little; maybe I'm lightly rubbing on her thigh. We're having a nice time, is the point. And I tell her that I am going to see someone I used to know soon. Then she starts in on me, just like that, about how we might as well not even be a couple because I don't include her in any of my plans.

"What are you talking about?" I say. "Where do you come up with this stuff, Kitten?" Kitten is the name I call her when I am trying to get her to relax.

"Who exactly are you going to see?" she says.

"I told you," I say. "It's just a guy I used to know. He was my stepdad for a while. It's nothing."

"Nothing?" she says. "I've never even heard you mention a stepdad before. If you loved me, don't you think I should know about a thing like that?"

"You're being crazy," I say, and probably pour myself a full glass of vodka and tonic. "Just calm down. It's not that big of a deal."

"You not loving me is a big fucking deal. I'm tired of it. We can't keep going on like this."

And this goes on for a few minutes, with me trying to get her to relax, until finally she pushes too much and I end up losing my temper.

"Jesus. Shut the fuck up," I say. "Christ, you have some fat arms."

And then I end up putting my fist through our flimsy bedroom wall, one more thing I need to get fixed, just the kind of thing I want to do after scrubbing someone else's shit off

29

toilets all day, and I tell her I'm through with her. Then she starts crying and curls up on the floor in front of the door like dog, and begs me not to go. She says she needs me. Says she can't go on without me.

The phone rang. Cotton's friend answered. "Baby, we could use some more smokes," he said into the receiver. He said something else about making sure the kids go to bed when they get home and then hung up.

"Your old lady and the kids supposed to be back soon?" Cotton said.

"Probably."

"Think about putting that whiskey away," Cotton said.

"Hell, I'll smash the woman over the head with this bottle if she's got a problem with it," he said, and then winked at me. Then he drank from the bottle. They smoked and let their ashes fall into the moose.

"How's your mother doing?" Cotton said to me.

"Fine," I said. "Got a new job. Working at a bank." I wasn't sure how much I should say on the subject.

"It was no walk on the beach," he said, "living with your mother."

He was right. It sure as hell was no walk on the beach for me. We had a window that was boarded up for an entire winter. A can of cranberry sauce got thrown through it one Thanksgiving. I don't remember what the fight was over; the cost of my mother's classes, Cotton losing another job, me losing my sneaker in the creek. Maybe all of it, maybe none of it. Fighting was something that just happened, like rain, or car payments.

I had to spend half my fifth-grade year wearing my black dress shoes to school, which were already at least a size too small, after I lost my sneaker in the creek. Me and some of the neighborhood kids formed what we called the A.B.S.F., or the Anti-Bitch Strike Force. We told each other and ourselves we were getting revenge on the assholes in the neighborhood, but I think there is just a natural instinct in boys to cause destruction when in groups. We would wear camouflage and throw eggs at their houses and put toilet-paper in their trees. Then we would hide out in the woods by the creek. Sometimes we'd stay there for hours. It kept us out of our own houses.

Cotton was glad I had taken an interest in the military. Something he had spent some time in during Vietnam, though he was never actually stationed there. He even bought me a mock M-16 pellet gun. He gave me a pocket knife, too. Told me to keep track of my kills by carving marks on the stock of my weapon.

My mother kicked Cotton out for the last time not long after that Thanksgiving. A few months, maybe. That was back when she was working a lot of doubles at the hospital, back when she was taking night classes, working toward a degree she'd never finish. She looked tired back then. She still looks tired, and now she looks old, but she carries herself differently. Her posture has gotten better with age, for one thing. She came home and found Cotton applying a full-nelson to me, my face pressed against our plastic-topped dinner table. He wasn't trying to hurt me, but my poor mother, how could she have known? Cotton had wrestled a bit in school, and liked showing me moves when my mother wasn't around. He'd been drinking a bit, which was normal, but he was in good spirits. Maybe he was being a little rough, but that was just how he moved.

"That is the last time you'll ever abuse me or my children," my mother said before even putting down her bottle of diet Pepsi. "Get out."

31

"Martha, shut up. You don't know what you're talking about," he said.

"Get out now, or I'll call the police. I swear to God," she said.

"We were playing, for Christ sakes. Tell her we were just playing," he said.

I was frozen. I didn't speak.

"Were you playing when you knocked my tooth out down in Laredo?" my mother said.

"Look," he said, "we were both really drunk. We both did some dumb things down there, Martha."

"You think I deserved to get my tooth punched out? Are you hearing yourself?"

"That's not what I said. Tell her that's not what I said," he said to me. I remember him looking me right in the eye, urging me to say something in his defense.

I looked down. I wanted to tell myself that I believed if Cotton left, things would change for the better. My mother's situation, mine and my sister's, maybe even his. But I believe I was aware even then how little we learn from our mistakes. I can't imagine even now what I could have said.

"Don't worry, you don't have to speak to him," my mother said to me. "You're done," she said to him.

"Martha," he said, but he left that night.

I heard a car pull up outside. Cotton's friend slid the bottle of whisky across the table to me. "You got kids," he said to me.

"No," I said.

"Don't," he said, as if it were the kind of thing I should trust his advice on.

The door banged open and in came his wife and two little girls, five and seven maybe, though I am no good at judging that sort of thing. The wife was a bony woman wearing a faded pink polo with an embroidered logo above one of the breasts that read *Fat Harold's Road House*. Probably a truck stop she waitresses at. She eyed the whisky, though she didn't say anything about it. Maybe she didn't want to start a fight in front of company. From my experience, people are less likely to fight in front of strangers than in front of children.

"I've had a long day," the wife said. And that I believed. Bags under her eyes as dark as the coffee stains on her shirt. "I'm going to get a shower and then I'm going to turn in for the night. Girls, get your jammies on and then get ready for bed, okay?" She flashed me a pleasant enough looking smile, but didn't seem interested in any introductions. She said goodnight to no one in particular, and her and the bigger of the two girls went off into other parts of the house.

The smaller girl climbed up on Cotton's lap.

"Did you see the picture I colored for you, Cotton?" the little girl said.

"I did," he said to her in a soft sort of way. He reached over his beer can and picked up the coloring book and held it so that the two of them could better see the picture. The pages shook a little in his hands. "Your daddy was showing it to me earlier. You did a beautiful job. I'll hang it on the fridge later so everyone can see how nice it is."

Cotton was smiling with her on his lap, as if this were his little girl. His own that he loved.

"I'm glad you like the picture," the little girl said to him.

"I do like it very much," he said. "But I think it is time for you to go night-night, Pumpkin." She kissed him on the forehead and climbed down from his lap. She said goodnight and picked up the pink stuffed toad near my feet and went off.

Her father reached across the table and picked up his Old Crow, took a big pull, and then handed it back to me.

Cotton looked up from the picture and his eyes met mine. The smile remained on his face.

I tried to think of something to say to him, but I kept thinking of the time he called me a pussy for not wanting to keep trying to learn to ride my bike, and how he told me to cut off my hands because they weren't good for anything. I tried to remember myself coloring a picture for him, and what he might have said at the time, but nothing came. Though surely there must have been moments like that. I thought about how he'll be dead soon and how he must have a lot of regrets. I thought about how when I got home, if I tried to tell my girlfriend about him, anything I'd say would make him sound pathetic. I thought about how maybe he made a difference in my life, and maybe I made a difference in his, but nothing I could say now would change anything. And I thought about my girlfriend, and that maybe I'd call in to work and take a day off, and take her for a drive, she'd like that, nowhere in particular, but maybe stop off at a small-town diner and get pie, but it wouldn't be as good as hers—and I'd be sure to let her know, and I know this would make her smile, but she'd be modest and say that she really isn't a very good cook—she's like that. Or maybe I'd just bring home a movie and a six-pack of something nice, she'd like that too. We'd have a nice time though.

Cotton finished his beer. He crushed the can and laid it on its side next to the moose.

"Will you grab me another? And get another for yourself if you want," he said.

Cotton, this other drunk, and I mostly sat in silence and drank our whiskey and tallboys. When I left, he told me he loved me. I said I loved him too. What else, really, could I say?

HOW DOLLY PARTON
RUINED MY LIFE

Last week me and my girlfriend Doreen were in Nashville. This week I've been spending a lot of time in the basement with her cat. I'm hoping whatever it is she's doing is just a fling.

We both had the weekend free, me and Doreen. I just lost my job at the cookie factory outside Paducah, and she took the weekend off to cheer me up. I got a case of Pabst Blue Ribbon for the road and we drove to Nashville. Why not Murfreesboro, or Clarksville, or even down to Chattanooga? I wish we went anywhere but Nashville. But she said, hey, let's go to Nashville, so we went.

We rented a room at Value Inn down on Wallace Road and I drank a beer and watched David Lee Roth make a nice bluff with pocket twos on the Celebrity Poker Tour while she showered and shaved her legs and armpits. She has beautiful armpits. I should have told her that.

I had another beer and then we drove downtown. We planned on going to a few bars and get a bite to eat, but we only made one stop. It was a tiny place off Second or Third, near where we parked. Maybe it was called The Black Lung, or maybe that's what Doreen said it should've been called. It wasn't much to look at. Old men sat at the bar and in pairs at a few wire-spool tables. The bartender was a heavyset guy in a black sleeveless shirt. His armpits were as unappealing as my Doreen's are beautiful. We might have left, I wish now that we had, but we noticed a band setting up on what was really more boards and pallets than a stage, and somehow I already had a beer in my hand, either from Doreen or by instinct, so we stayed.

I was glad to be spending time with Doreen in Nashville. And it was nice of Doreen to want to do something to cheer me up, though truth be told, losing the job felt like a blessing in most ways I saw it. But there had been something on my mind for a couple weeks. Something that I couldn't shake out of my head. Something that made me think Doreen had another reason for taking me to Nashville. I thought maybe she had something important she wanted to tell me. Something, you know, that I might not actually want to hear. I thought she might be lubing up my nerves like that time she took me to that Rush concert before telling me that she broke the pipe that my buddy Mikey made from the head of a cigar-store Indian.

The thing that I couldn't get out of my head happened a couple weeks before when me and Mikey were drinking Pabst in the basement. Doreen came down. She said she was looking for the iron or the cat or something. I saw Mikey looking at her belly. Truth is she had been getting a little fat in the belly. But let me tell you, I honestly think that can be a sexy thing on a woman. And then Mikey said to me, "Jesus, she's not pregnant is she?"

It made me uncomfortable, him staring at her belly like that. So I asked her to go to the store to pick up more Pabst and some of those cheddar-filled pretzels. But after that I couldn't get the idea out of my head. And then she decides to go to Nashville all of a sudden. What's a guy to think?

Doreen sat us at one of the wire-spools near the band. They didn't look like much. A guitarist, a fiddle player, and a chick with an autoharp. They didn't even have a drummer. I had been a drummer in a rock band when Doreen and I met. She liked rocker guys, but I'm not going to say she was a groupie. She was the kind of girl usually reserved for lead singers. Hot. Like my buddy Mikey says, like-a-pussy-glued-to-a-building-on-fire hot. You should know my buddy Mikey. He's a lead singer. The kind of guy who sticks nails up his nose and waxes his body hair. The kind of guy who would build a pipe out of the head of a cigar-store Indian. A natural entertainer. I left my band when I got a promotion at the cookie factory and had to start working weekends. Like I said, Doreen always liked rocker guys, but I guess that shows how people change.

The band played what I figured were cover songs. Not that I know many country songs, but they sounded like things I've heard. The girl with the autoharp sang. She wasn't bad-looking, maybe a little horse-faced, but not bad. She had a killer voice. Could hit high notes like Axl Rose. So we sat there and listened and had a couple more beers. At first, I took that Doreen was drinking as a good sign that she wasn't pregnant. But then I thought it was just as likely that she was pregnant and she was drinking to make me think that she wasn't. I had no way of knowing for sure. Then she wanted to talk about what I might do about work. She said her dad could use a hand putting shingles on roofs until I could figure something else out. I told her maybe I'd start another band. Maybe I'd play drums for this country band. It's time for something new, I told her. I'll admit I was drunk.

The band started playing "I Will Always Love You." That one I recognized because it came on the radio while me and Doreen were making out in my Ranchero on our first date

37

almost four years ago. She had reached over and turned the volume up, and I took that to mean something. I looked over at Doreen and thought about that night and these white and gold knee-high boots she wore. Those boots must have taken me twenty minutes to unlace. And I wondered if she still had them somewhere. Then I see there is this other lady up on the stage and I don't know where she came from. Believe me, if she had been hanging around the bar when we came in I would have noticed. And this wasn't the kind of place with a dressing room or backstage. Maybe she had been hanging around in the pisser. She was older, with a big chest, but good looking for her age.

I wasn't sure then, but I'm sure now. It was Dolly Parton.

So Doreen and I were at the table closest to the stage, and Dolly Parton and this slightly horse-faced girl were singing a duet to "I Will Always Love You." I am embarrassed to admit this next part. Dolly was staring right at us while singing, giving this look. I even checked behind us to make sure it wasn't someone else she was singing to, giving this look to. I've been around enough bands to know what those kind of looks mean. I looked at Doreen, and she looked at me and took my hand and placed it on the soft rayon of the stocking that clenched her thigh, and I said to her, "You better be careful, baby. Dolly is up there giving me the eye. She's old but she's still got an ass that'd make the Dalai Lama horny." Knowing what I now know, I feel stupid for having said that. But who knows why we say what we say? When you're in love, when you're intimate, you say things.

After the band finished their set, I bought the horse-faced girl a beer and told her I thought she was good. I told her about how I was a drummer and I was looking for a group to join.

Doreen came over and put her arm around me. She said, "I don't know, I don't think your red-leather-tiger-striped pants and double bass drum would go very well with this kind of music."

"Shit, Doreen," I said. "I'm talking business."

"Oh, I'm sorry," she said. "You're talking business. That must mean it's none of my business, right?" She's like that. Has a clever comment for everything. Smart girl.

So I walked her over near the pisser for a little privacy. And that's when I said it. Believe me, I wish that I hadn't. "Baby, what's this all about? Just tell me. Are you pregnant?" That look that held on her face has been burning in my head ever since. It was a mix of I want to punch your teeth out and something else. Maybe disappointment. Maybe acceptance. I've seen a lot of her looks. I thought I'd seen them all. But that was a new one. And then she turned and went into the pisser. I knew she was upset, but still I called after her, "Baby, when you're done in the can, grab me another beer, I got no cash left." Who knows why we say what we say.

I went back to talking to the horse-faced girl. After a while I saw that Doreen was sitting with Dolly. They were doing double shots together. I figured, hell, she could use another woman to talk to. I was glad she was talking to Dolly instead of any of the back-haired hicks hanging out in the joint. I've dated girls like that. Girls that would hang all over the fattest, most tattooed, most likely-just-out-of-prison guy in the bar to make you jealous. That's one of the things, one of the many many things, I love about Doreen. She wasn't into putting on a show.

Me and the horse-face girl had another beer. She told me her name was Roxy and I gave her my number. I told her I was available anytime. I told her I was free to travel. I told her I was versatile.

I figured Doreen would've been calmed down by then. And that we could go back to the Value Inn and make love, and then maybe drink champagne or something nice. Something as sort of an apology for what I said. But Doreen was gone. Roxy said she saw her and her friend leave together. I asked her if Doreen looked upset when she was leaving. She said she would keep in touch.

The band played another set and I waited for Doreen. By then a couple of weathered-looking ladies appeared in the bar. One of them was dancing closely over in a corner with a guy with arms as hairy as a Saint Bernard. I never slow-danced with Doreen. I kept waiting. I waited for Doreen to come back. I waited until the bartender with the unappealing armpits said I couldn't wait anymore. And then I waited in the parking lot until the sun rose.

Things have been bad for me since Doreen left. Every morning more of my own hair has shed on my pillow. It sheds on her pillow too. I can hardly eat, and when I do stomach something, it's been crisp rice. But I still have hope. She has to come back. Something has to be done about her stuff. What kind of woman would leave her cat? Sure, Dolly Parton has money, but money can't buy everything. Money can't buy that pink and brown afghan that her grandmother knitted. Her grandmother is dead after all. Money can't buy the picture I have on the nightstand of her as a girl on her daddy's farm, feeding a can of beer to her pig. She has to come back. For her stuff if nothing else. Maybe then I can tell her everything I should have told her before, about how she has nice armpits and how I like her belly.

I spend most of my time these days sitting in the basement drinking Pabst with the cat, writing songs for Doreen. As a drummer, it's the kind of thing I'm new at. Mikey tells me the songs have potential.

A TERRIBLE SOUND

This place has no limes, no celery stalks, no pull-tab tickets, not even smoke since it's technically a government building. But it suits me fine because it's dark, and I drink beer, haven't gambled in years, and never have cared for cigarettes. She's drunk again, but she orders another double Jack, neat, and gets me a can of Tui. She's a pretty girl who likes scarves and smells like the holidays. Her name's Daisy, she has a degree in art history from some school I've never heard of in Portland, and she's washing dishes down here at McMurdo Station, Antarctica. She's not special in that regard—this place is full of people just like her—but she's special in the fact that, for whatever reason, she chooses to talk to me.

"I used to go camping with my Uncle Butch and my dad every summer at this run-down campground," she says. "There were signs all over telling you not to feed the chipmunks. One summer when I was eight or nine, Uncle Butch lured these chipmunks over near us, like five of them, with popcorn." She's a close talker when she's been drinking, or maybe she's always a close talker for all I know, but she scoots in closer to me and our knees are touching, which is something I am so aware of it's hard for me to pay attention to what she's telling me.

"He kept doing this all night. These chipmunks were hanging out with us listening to Uncle Butch tell stories, the same stories he always told, about the Navy and being drunk on a beach in Haiti with a couple of what must have been hookers, building sandcastles all night. These cute little guys are right over near us, and I start feeding them too. They were the most adorable things I'd ever seen. Then the next thing you know, my dad pours hot coffee all over one of their heads. You should have heard the terrible sound he made." Not only is she a close talker, but now she puts her hand on my shoulder. She'd probably be looking me in the eyes, but I'm scared if I make eye contact she'll see things in me she doesn't like. "Isn't that a terrible thing to do?"

I tell her I hate coffee.

She's joined me nearly every night here at the bar for the last month and has told me all sorts of things about herself. She's told me about how she got that J-shaped scar on her neck from a spider bite when she was thirteen and how a boyfriend freshman year in college used to cover it with his hand during sex. And she's told me about growing up Catholic, and her dad's porn collection, and about how much she likes making macaroni pictures.

I don't remember ever making macaroni pictures, and though I've been familiar with porn and Catholicism, I don't have much to say on the subjects, but she keeps telling me things, which is good because I'm not good at communicating. Mostly I don't know what to talk about around women, except for my wife, who I don't tell her about. I don't tell her we've been married for the past fourteen years but are now separated. Let's call my wife Maggie—no, let's call her Sam.

I don't tell her how Sam played professional roller derby until she tore an ACL three years into our marriage. I don't tell her how Sam was roller-skating when we met, roller-skating in the parking lot of a Piggly Wiggly with this other girl, a big-chested redhead who would years later threaten to kill me with a broken Labatt bottle. I was on my way to pick up some butter or cigarettes for my mother when I saw them. It was the most innocent-looking thing. Two young women in skirts and ponytails, laughing the way only girls on roller skates can laugh. I imagined they smelled like bubblegum and went to church. They were the kind of girls you'd see in an ad for juice boxes, the kind of girls I'd like to talk to, only I didn't make much conversation then either. So I walked toward the entrance to the Piggly Wiggly but didn't take my eyes off them. And then I stepped in front of a truck.

I was on the ground and must have been dazed for a moment until I heard a woman's voice yell, "Watch where the fuck you are going, cocksucker." I imagined it was the driver of the truck advising me. But when I got my bearings, I saw it was the big-chested redhead speaking with the driver.

I looked up and the sun was bright in my eyes. Maybe my vision was blurry from the impact, but when my eyes focused, I was surprised to see the other girl, the one I would marry, standing over me like an angel, or maybe the opposite of an angel. Her face was dark with thick make-up, her knees and elbows were scabby like a clumsy toddler's, and her arms had words written on them in black, sweat-smeared marker: "Fuck You" on her left arm and "Fuck God" on her right. It was stupid and the sort of thing meant for attention, but she was beautiful and I was in love.

"Hey, you. You okay?" she said.

I was, but I worried if I was, she would leave. I said, "What happened?"

"You got plowed by a fucking truck, man," she said. "Hey, Dee Dee. This guy seems kind of out of it."

"You better hope he's okay, asshole," the girl called Dee Dee said to the driver. "If he's not, you'll be shitting out this skate."

I feared if I didn't get up, she'd hold true to her words, so I stood. The girls were impressed with my resilience. They took me out for some beers at a bar full of guys with arms as thick as my neck and women with arms as thick as my neck. I was twenty-two, had recently flunked out of college for the second time, lived with my mother in the house I was raised in, and was wearing a sweater I'd had since high school that had a picture of a reindeer on it. But two beautiful women were buying me drinks, so you think I'd be feeling good, and I was, but part of me expected the worst, that they'd invited me here as a trick, that any minute some goon with an American flag tattooed on his bald head would take away my pants or shoes.

We drank pitchers of beer. They told me they thought my reindeer sweater was adorable, and they drew a roller skate on my neck with a magic marker. I don't remember what we talked about, but it was more important than the weather, or maybe it was the weather, but I remember they laughed at things I said, and we played "Time After Time," over and over again on the jukebox. And for the first time in my life I danced with someone besides myself in front of the mirror, and I felt I could become a new person, someone who didn't need college, who could change motor oil by himself, who could walk into a bar in the middle of Phoenix or Detroit or Scott City and not feel self-conscious about my skinny arms or fat belly and be comfortable enough to talk to beautiful women—or ugly women for that matter if I wanted—and be the kind of guy who tells the kind of guy who says things to women like "you got a nice ass" to have some fucking respect.

And afterward Sam came home with me to my mother's house, and we made love in the same bed I'd slept in for a decade. She had cigarette burns on her ass, and it made me think it must have been a conscious effort on her part to go home with a guy like me, someone who wouldn't scar her ass. And she stayed over nearly every night for three weeks until my mother lent us the money to get a place of our own, a tiny apartment above a hardware store where I'd spend my mornings talking to the owner, learning how to do things like caulk tubs and replace electrical outlets.

But I don't tell any of this to Daisy.

I work at the wastewater treatment plant here at McMurdo, monitoring the station and flushing treated waste back out into the ocean underneath a sheet of ice five feet thick. I also filter large untreatable things from the tank like tampons, big chunks of corn, and condoms. This, I've told Daisy about. And for the last couple weeks she's been flushing letters down the toilet enclosed in condoms. It's given me something to look forward to.

The condom messages tell me things she'd like me to do to her or things that she'd like to do to me—things that involve ice and scarves, things that involve positions I'm not familiar with or capable of. I'd like to believe she means every word she's written, but she doesn't say these things in person, so maybe she's just trying to give me a thrill or provide community service for a lonely guy. I know myself and I know my odds; I know I have been blessed once already in my life with a woman far out of my league, so it's hard for me to believe what she writes in these messages.

She knocks back the rest of her Jack, and it's my turn for the next round, but some Air Force guy steps in between us so that his ass is touching my knee. He has probably been waiting right behind her for fifteen minutes, watching for the moment she puts her empty glass down. He pays no attention to me.

"What'll you be having, sweetheart," he says as though she has no other option than to have something.

She gives me a look, and I don't know what it means, if it means anything. Maybe she wants me to intervene in some way, or maybe not, but I don't know how to react, so I don't. Nonetheless, I am surprised when she tells the guy she'll have another double Jack.

No one here much likes the military guys. They have the wrong mentality for the place—too macho, too exclusive, except when they are at the bar making passes at women. They try the same shit they try to pick up women in Seoul or Manila, except they fail miserably nearly every time here, because in a place where three out of every four people are guys, there is no reason for a pretty girl to fall for that.

The Air Force guy turns and acknowledges my presence. "Can't a guy get some service from this menopausal bitch?" He's talking about this evening's bartender, Janet, who is also McMurdo's hairstylist and someone I eat breakfast with on occasion, but I don't oppose his comment. He's a tall guy with a square head, the kind of guy you'd know was in the military even if you didn't know he was in the military. He's wearing a shirt with the phrase "I Make Good Babies" across the front. He's younger than me but strikes me as too old to wear a shirt like that, and I can't help but think of what a kick Sam would have gotten out of this guy and his stupid shirt. We would have laughed about it later in the night, and while we were kissing but before we made love she probably would have said to me, "Wait. Do you make good babies?"

I take a twenty out of my wallet, and when Janet comes around she takes my order before she takes the makes-good-babies guy's. I order drinks for me and Daisy, and I don't know why I do it, but I ask Janet to get the guy a drink, too. He orders the worst kind of beer on station, CD, three-years-old, flat, tastes like metal, the beer anyone who has been around here any time at all knows better than to order. He nods in appreciation but then turns back toward Daisy. I wonder if it is obvious Daisy and I aren't a couple or if this guy just doesn't care.

My brother Jackie is in the Army. He's a major and works at a desk in D.C. now. He's married to a Japanese woman, has twin boys who are all-district cross-country runners, drives a half-ton Ford pick-up, and has a globe in his living room made out of things like gold and quartz. I paid him a visit a couple years back, right before I first came down here.

"Michael," he told me over coffee one morning, "I think this change will be good for you."

I was surprised when he joined ROTC as a sophomore in college. Before that he had played the bass guitar in a funk band called Booty Squad. Sometimes people change for the better, and sometimes they just do different things. I have found myself surprised by what we're capable of. My brother is responsible for the deaths of dozens of people. I've seen the awards and certificates that prove it. Me, I'm capable of punching a woman in the stomach.

The Air Force guy introduces himself to Daisy as Rock, probably short for where he's from, Rockford or something, or probably no one calls him that at all. It's a name both so stupid and fitting I can't help but laugh out loud. Neither of them pays attention to me.

"What's your name, sweetheart," he says, and when she tells him, he says she is as pretty as a flower, though I somehow doubt this guy really finds beauty in flowers.

Another Air Force guy, seeing his buddy is having some luck, starts hanging around us like a hyena, waiting for Rock to strike out or hoping Daisy has a friend besides me. He's standing there waiting with a stupid grin that makes me think of a used-car salesman. He's got a face like Abraham Lincoln, but it's obvious even he has more confidence than me. And I imagine, as sad as it is, his waiting game has worked for him at least once in his life.

Me and Sam used to sit in the back of bars and watch other couples or potential couples and make up stories about them, where they've been, where they're going.

"See that couple at the end of the bar," she might say, "the older guy with the frosted tips and the girl in the denim jacket. She's his law partner's daughter. They came to this shithole so no one from the firm would see them. They stopped off at J.C. Penney on the way and he bought that leather jacket to fit in with the rough crowd here. Not a crease or scratch on it."

"What about his boots," I might say.

"She had him give some guy in the parking lot 200 dollars for them."

"Come on. She had him do it?"

"Yeah, you can tell she's in control. She's done the seducing, probably a way to get back at Daddy for years of violin lessons. Look at how much she's touching him. It can't be completely sincere. There's no way a girl that pretty could be into a guy with frosted tips."

Sometimes we'd go home and have the kind of sex we thought these couples would have. But often we'd be too drunk and would fall asleep in each other's arms after sloppily kissing and unsuccessfully fumbling with the belt under her fattening belly. But let me tell you, that's real love—when you still wake up satisfied the next morning when your face is pressed into her armpit and the smell of her drool makes you happy.

But we were fighting more and more. It doesn't matter what the fights were about, just that any conversation when we were drunk enough had the potential to take that turn. A lot of it came down to one of us trying to make the other feel as bad as we felt at the time. This one time—and I don't know what the fight was over but I don't think it was any more spectacular than the others—I punched her in the stomach. I'd like to say I don't remember doing that, but I do remember, and I remember that something about it felt natural, and I knew I had crossed a line, and now that I was the kind of guy who would punch a woman, there would never be a more fitting way to describe me.

Rock is saying something into Daisy's ear. I can't hear what it is, but I imagine and hope it is something rude. I hope he crosses the line and asks her about making good babies or if her scarf matches her panties. He is close enough to me that I can smell him, and he smells too good to be here. We work hard and don't shower often. The National Science Foundation asks this of us. We grow used to it. No need for cologne or high-endurance body wash, but he smells like a fucking sixteen-year-old on his way to homecoming. Apparently he hasn't crossed the line yet because she smiles at whatever he tells her and then says something back that means nothing to me, the name of a store or a species of tropical bird maybe. Now I am feeling like a creep, like this other Air Force guy, Lincoln, who's also still watching the two of them. It crosses my mind to buy him a beer.

"CDs for everyone," I tell Janet.

Lincoln nods in appreciation, and then his eyes are back on Daisy and Rock. My eyes go back to them, too. He's moved closer to her, but she hasn't moved an inch.

"So who's this guy?" Rock says to Daisy about me. "Your boss or your dad or something?" His laugh sounds like a worn fan belt.

"He's a pen pal," she says. That comment should be flattering given the condom messages, but I can't imagine it sounds flattering about me to Rock, which is maybe more important.

It's guys like this I used to imagine mistreated women.

This one night a couple years ago, me and Sam were drunk, of course, drunk on fine beer from some wine bar downtown, Belgian beer that smelled like cherries and earth. They were wonderful, but we had a fight. Why is it that your worst nights happen on the nights you try hardest to make nice? Even if I remembered what the particular fight was over, there is no point in elaborating on my meanness any further. I'll tell you it was raining and I ended up locked out of the house. I stood in the yard yelling, punching our birch tree until my hand bled, apologizing, telling her I could cook like a Polish grandmother for fuck's sake. And then I apologized more, and then I yelled some more. Eventually I fell asleep in the rain. What kind of wild animal exists that doesn't even have enough sense to get out of the rain?

Let me say that usually after nights like that neither of us were still upset or embarrassed—we would just go on living, I'd still hold her hand in line at the store, and she'd still rub my neck while we watched game shows after work. But the morning after that fight, when I walked through the unlocked door, wet and feeling like I was hit by a truck, Sam was sitting at the kitchen table, not looking upset but looking like something—I still can't describe it, but it wasn't sad and wasn't good.

"We'll be miserable with or without each other," she told me, "but if we go on, we'll kill each other."

She didn't leave that day, or even the next day, but I knew things were over. And she was right about the miserable part.

Rock unlaces the scarf from Daisy's neck—his fingers are meatier than my thumbs—and strings it around his own. This makes Daisy smile.

"I don't know why you've been depriving the world of seeing something so beautiful as your neck," Rock says. This makes Daisy smile too.

She's getting dangerously drunk, but the thing is there is no dangerously drunk here. All the dorms are a couple hundred yards or so from the bar. It is continuously high noon. It is the safest place on Earth.

The bar is starting to get crowded—it usually does near last call—with some people desperately searching for companionship and others desperately avoiding it. Janet is pouring drinks generously and people here appreciate that. It is the saddest place on Earth.

Rock tells Daisy about all the great places he's seen serving Uncle Sam, beautiful beaches in Japan and Guam, and then says to her, "I've got a few beers over in 202. You want to get out of here?" He takes a step back from the bar, prepared to leave. So much confidence. "I also got some Habu sake a buddy of mine shipped down from Okinawa. Just wait till you hear the stories I have involving that shit."

Something comes over me, and I say, "The thing about shit...."

Rock stops talking and they all turn, their eyes fixed on me, waiting for what I'll say next. And I wait, too, until I realize there is absolutely nothing else I want to say.

Then Daisy puts a hand back on my shoulder. I still can't bring myself to look directly into her face, so instead I look at the scar on her neck. It makes me think about the scar that ran the length of Sam's knee and about how often I would touch it, even years after surgery, and how a reminder of someone's pain makes it somehow easier to love them. And I have the desire to run my fingers along Daisy's scar, but I know I would feel ridiculous doing it, even though I could see someone like Rock doing it and saying something like "What happened here? You get a hickey from an angel?" and it seeming normal.

And then I realize her hand is on my shoulder so she can balance herself as she stands. She leans in closer to me and says, "Keep an eye out for another letter."

She doesn't wait for my response, and as I watch her and Rock walk out together into the sunshine, her leaning into him with her arm around his waist for stability, I lay money on the bar for one more drink and do my best not to think about what'll go on when they get to 202. I don't know if he'll be gentleman enough to offer the drink he promised, if he'll rub his fingers across her scar, or if he'll cover it with his hand. I do know I will be right here tomorrow, in this exact seat, waiting.

BLUE STAR

There are no bars in Kotzebue, which made me hesitate when she asked if I wanted to do something. The sores on her lip and the rate of STDs in this town made me hesitate too, but I've worked three weeks straight, haven't seen anything other than my apartment and the hospital where I work, and have barely met anyone besides coworkers, patients, and the posse of ravens that perch on the dumpster outside my window. So we are walking along the frozen Chukchi Sea, a case of Keystone Ice in tow for us to split. Even gloved, my fingers are starting to numb.

"Drink a little more and your blood will flow better," she says. "You won't get frostbite."

"I don't think that's how it works," I say.

She works at Registration, but she's late nearly every day, sometimes by hours. Most locals are. The sun barely rises either, so I might not hold sense of timing against them except there's a line at the only liquor store every day when it opens, still pitch dark.

She's two beers in and beginning to wobble. I don't think we should go further, so I reach for her hand, pull her to a stop. She turns and kisses me. Bites my lip. Her breath might be the only smell not trapped by the ice and snow for a mile—it's musty, like wet wool and roast beef, makes me think of my dead grandma. I'm five beers in, but that's not enough to make me forget about those sores on her lip.

I step back and put my hand to her face, brush her dark hair behind her shoulder. I've noticed the tattoo on her neck before, but I study it now in the blue glow of the arctic night. It says *Barney*. The ink has severely bled.

"Tell me about this," I say, rubbing it.

"An old woman in Kobuk does them. Uses bird bones and sinew. Soot and urine. Hurts like shit. Supposed to prepare girls for childbirth."

My dad had been a tattooist in Buffalo. If I'd been a sentimental drunk sooner, I might have gotten to know him. Instead, I sat around a few months back with someone who had.

"Back then you'd use the same needle on everyone till it dulled," the lady had said. She rolled up her sleeve and showed me a tattoo faded deep under her skin, like veins. "He made the nautical star famous, your father. One night a couple us dykes came into his shop. We wanted a symbol, left with blue stars on our wrists. Nowadays there's more stars on skin than in the Milky Way."

Tonight in Kotzebue, I imagine I can see each star in the Milky Way. She pushes my hand off her neck and walks deeper out to sea. From here I'm told it's 200 miles to Russia, 150 miles to the international dateline. This girl keeps walking, might walk right to tomorrow. I call after her. I follow.

BLESSED

So my sister's boyfriend Connor, the father of her three-year-old Toby, gets out of a thirty-day detox center the other day. What gets me is that everyone, and by everyone I mean my mom and my mom's boyfriend Carl, thinks it's just great, his effort to get clean. As if his other times in and out of these type of places, and his failure to ever stay sober before, don't mean anything now. As if, regardless of whether or not he were an addict, he weren't also an asshole. Truth is this guy doesn't have it in him to stay clean. And thirty-day detox centers don't mean shit for long-term recovery anyway, which is a different matter altogether, but not a matter worth going into now.

This kid Toby, this nephew of mine, I've avoided him as much as I could until just recently. I've avoided seeing him. I've avoided talking about him. I've avoided hearing about him and the kinds of little Caterpillar-brand shoes and plastic dump trucks my mom and Carl get for him. I've had a lot of bad days dealing with my sister and her being involved with types like Connor, not that I've thought of her as innocent for a long time, so when she wound up pregnant by him that was it for me. I didn't want to have anything to do with that situation.

But then one day a couple weeks ago I was walking to work up Spenard, a day when it seemed no one else was appreciating the sunshine, and I saw a sign on the number 36 bus. I don't know, it was probably for domestic violence awareness, or maybe it was an underwear ad. But it had this teenage girl on it, thick black hair tangled like an arbor knot, and these horrified and avoiding eyes, like as if they were watching kittens falling from the sky and splattering on roofs and pavement all around her. I know it was just a stupid ad, and the girl was just a model, but still I couldn't help but feel sorry for someone with eyes like that, real or not. So I've been making an effort.

What really gets me, though, is that first day out of detox and Connor says about how much he misses and loves my sister and how he needs to spend alone time with her. It seems to me that if you haven't seen your own son in thirty days, maybe your top priority would be spending quality with him. Or them both. Together. Like a family. He says he wants to take her down to Homer for the weekend, do some fishing and whatnot, though I am sure my sister will foot the bill since the guy doesn't have it in him to do steady work.

My mom and Carl already had weekend plans to go to a snow globe convention in North Pole, so my sister asked me to watch Toby. Part of me would have liked to say no, because I don't want them getting to the point where they try taking advantage. Dropping the kid off at my place randomly so they could do God knows what. But I also knew the kind of dirtball they'd end up sticking him with if I said no.

I went by my sister's place to pick the kid up because I didn't want to chance it that Connor might step foot in my place. I don't trust the guy. I wouldn't doubt that he'd slip my Clash forty-fives under his shirt, or leave a window unlocked for the next time he goes on a binge, which he will, not that you need to dislike someone to steal their stuff.

My sister, God love her, is not a bright girl. She has the vocabulary of a concussed parrot. Despite this, she is doing well for herself. She is a good-looking girl, which is something I have heard about more than I care to say since she was in junior high. She is an assistant manager at a boutique in the Dimond Center, and if she is qualified to do one thing in this world, and I mean this in the most loving way, it is selling translucent plastic jewelry.

There are a lot of things in this world I don't fully understand, and one of them is why my sister lets guys like Connor drag her down. I've heard from here and there about her getting smacked around. Believe me, there are things inside of me I'd like to let come out. But it wouldn't change anything between the two of them.

When I got to my sister's place the three of them were waiting outside, no doubt impatiently, by her Jetta. If I didn't know them I might have thought they looked like a nice young family. The kind that gives you hope for our generation. Connor, who was uncommonly clean-shaven and smelled like a broken bottle of Old Spice, reached out to shake my hand. I didn't want to cause a scene in front of the kid, so I accepted his hand, which jitters, even though he is twenty-seven, like a frozen-daiquiri machine. This next part I saw coming because it is the kind of thing he has said to me almost every time I have seen him in the last few years.

"Thirty-one days sober," he said. Then he went into the other thing I am tired of hearing him say. "Look, I know you don't think much of me. I don't blame you. But I am off everything right now. I want to do right by your sister and my son. This time is different. Please believe me."

No one in the world with any sense would believe him, again, God love my sister, and I would have liked to tell him so, but also again, no reason to do so in front of Toby. "Right on," is what I said instead.

57

Connor lit a Marlboro and gave me a smile. He has this way about smiling as if there is some kind of joke we are in on together. It bothers me. I wanted to get the kid and go before Connor tried making any more small talk. He's the kind of guy who will give you his opinion on everything if he's got the chance. As if you give a shit about his opinion. As if being a junkie, a self-proclaimed recovering one, somehow gives him the right.

"And I'm done cheating on your sister too," he told me. "I don't deserve the chances she's given me. It's like I'm blessed."

I really couldn't care less about all that, unless of course, that is the reason she decides to leave him, which it won't be, because it has been going on like this for years.

Toby was playing with the shoelace of one of his dad's filthy Airwalks. I would have liked to think this kid had sense enough to dislike this guy too, but I knew that wasn't the case. I've known Connor a long time, years before my sister got involved with him, and there's something about him other people find likeable, at least at first. He's always been loved by women. And the couple of times I've seen him with Toby, the kid adores him. What more could anyone want in this world than to be loved?

My sister removed the car seat from her car and started buckling it into the back seat of my New Yorker. Toby must have realized his parents were leaving him with me and started a screaming fit that made it sound as if he had swallowed a razor blade. My sister hugged the kid and made some kind of noises to him that made me think of tropical birds while Connor got into the driver's seat of her Jetta and started the engine.

One summer when I was twelve and my sister was nine our parents sent us to stay with our grandmother in a cottage up on Lake Ontario. We'd swim, and climb trees, and sink cans with stones into the lake. The whole summer, me and her. Late

August, shortly before we went back to our parents, we walked through an orchard, stopping once in a while to pick an apple and eat it, even though they weren't quite ripe. The sky darkened and before long rain was coming down in gallons. Even so, even with the chill of late summer upstate New York rain matting our filthy clothes and hair to our skin, we weren't in a hurry to be anywhere else. At one point a dog started following us. I thought it might be a watch dog for the orchard, but it was too small and too fat. We walked and our shoes squished in the soft orchard grass and the dog followed us. After a while I faced the dog and knelt down and held a hand towards it. "Do you have some place you have to be, dog?" I said. I don't know what kind of dog it was, but it didn't look like any kind I'd want to have. I reached my hand further towards its face and noticed it had long nipples and a saggy belly. I looked back to tell my sister that it was pregnant, and right then it lunged and nipped a couple of my fingers, and then my sister moved in front of me and kicked it in the stomach. The dog yelped and ran behind one of the apple trees. I was twelve and bleeding and suddenly cold, so pregnant or not, felt no sympathy for the dog. But my sister, God love her, knelt in the grass and mud and wept like an infant. The rain let up, the sun broke through the clouds and brought that earthy after-rain smell, and my clothes felt heavier by the minute. "Come on, let's get back. Grandmom will worry," I finally said. But it was a long time before she would rub the mud off her palms and budge.

My sister gave Toby a fat, orange bracelet she was wearing and got him calmed down enough to buckle him in. She kissed him on the forehead and Connor flicked his cigarette out the window and honked the horn.

"All right," my sister said to me. "We'll give you a call Sunday night when we get back in town. Or you can always call my cell if you need anything." And she gave me a smile. But it was the kind of smile women at these boutiques use.

I saw Connor almost die once. We were at a party out at Donna Sikorski's who lived in a trailer with her older brother. At these kind of parties Connor would sometimes piss in a half-empty whiskey bottle and see how many people he could get to drink from it. I never want to think about it too hard, but I am sure I have had that guy's piss in my mouth. Friend or not, he's one of those guys I always felt on edge around. But he used to look out for me, and that's the kind of thing that goes a long way.

A few of us were standing around the kitchen passing a joint we got from Donna's brother, Northern Lights or something good like that. And then Jamie Warner, a nice-looking freshman, a little heavy in the waist, a girl I didn't know very well and probably wouldn't remember her name except for what happened next, came in through the front door, didn't say a word, and walked up right behind Connor, who was standing in front of me, and ran an opened pocket knife across his throat. He put his hand to his throat real quick like he had been bit by a mosquito and turned around. "What the fuck?" is the only thing he said. When he took his hand away from his throat and saw the blood, he sat down on the floor and touched his hand to his neck again. It seemed like everyone was frozen. Maybe no one knew what to do, but I don't think that was it. And I don't think it was that no one cared, though I couldn't have blamed anyone if that were the case. I just think the thing didn't seem real. Like everyone was trying to decide if it was a dream or not. Jamie had walked right back out the front door. No one tried to stop her, and no one called the police.

I was the one that finally took off my shirt and held it to his neck. And I was the one that drove him to the hospital, and remembering thinking while helping him out of my car in front of the emergency room that there was no way a human body could hold as much blood as was soaked into my seat.

I don't know why that girl tried to kill him. There were rumors about a pregnancy, and rumors about a rape, and rumors about Connor kicking her dad's teeth out. The truth might be in there somewhere.

Connor would later tell countless lies about how he got that scar on his neck. I don't trust a word that comes out of that guy's mouth. The lies about sobriety, the lies about my sister. But there's a part of me that can't blame him. There are things I've done that are hard to admit even to myself.

I pulled out of my sister's complex onto Muldoon. The kid was still sobbing. I didn't know where to take him, so I drove with no place in mind, hoping he'd stop. I wondered how long he could keep it up, and I knew if he was as stubborn as either of his parents we might wind up in Canada before he quit, or fell asleep, or something.

I could see his mother and his father in his face as he cried. I know people argue that a kid needs to be raised this way or that way. But I couldn't help but wonder as I watched the kid, if any of that really matters.

SIDESHOW

I had just started a new job selling magazine subscriptions door to door. It wasn't much of a job. No regular pay, just a small commission. But I was a month sober at that time, and it was better than what I had been doing, which was nothing. It wasn't something I was good at. Maybe I didn't have the patience, or the sharp tongue, or the ability to read people, or whatever it is that real sales people have. It was something I took to start getting back on my feet if you can relate to that.

It was my second or third day working, and I was walking a neighborhood full of two-car garages, and mailboxes in the shape of things like roosters and boats. Sweat was beginning to soak through my shirt. I could smell myself.

I had seen a couple of kids go into this one house. It was the middle of the day when kids should be in school. I followed them and knocked on the door. When they answered I told them I was with the school system, that if they didn't go back their parents would be notified. A heavyset kid with a buzzcut who reminded me of a woodchuck told me they got out early on the account of a bomb threat. He said it was a good thing they were home because I was probably looking for houses to break into. I told him he was right, that no one expects it in the middle of the day. I said if they needed a job to look me up, that no one would expect kids either. I gave them a name that wasn't mine.

The house next door had rose bushes on the front lawn with black gravel over the soil as shiny as glass. The thought crossed my mind to pick a rose for Janine, my ex-girlfriend, but I didn't. I knocked on the door of that house instead. An older guy, maybe in his sixties, answered. He was in a burgundy bathrobe. I shook his hand and was startled. I might have taken a step back. Each of his hands had only two big fingers. They looked like lobster claws. Lobster claws made out of flesh.

"Please come in," he said. "It's so hot outside."

"Thank you," I said. I followed him in. I was glad to see what kind of home someone with hands like that would have. The place was clean and orderly like the yard. The chair and sofa had matching floral patterns. The kind old ladies and men with cats have.

"Please have a seat," he said. "Make yourself comfortable. May I get you anything, a glass of water, a beer?"

"Sure, water would be good," I said.

For the last few months I'd been having problems going to the bathroom. I'd have to piss all the time and couldn't hold it. The first time it happened I pissed my pants at a Seven-Eleven. I ended up pouring a Big Gulp down the front of my pants hoping everyone would think it was just slushy, not piss. Janine saw the whole thing.

The problem has been getting better lately, but I asked where the bathroom was just to be safe.

"Down the hall and on the left," he said. "Please make yourself comfortable."

He went to the kitchen for the drinks, and I went and checked out the bathroom. It was all done up in reds and gold.

Red basin, gold faucet. Red toilet, gold flusher. The toilet had one of those cushiony seats. This guy was doing all right for himself. I flushed the toilet and opened the medicine cabinet. I couldn't believe it, he had dental floss. Couldn't be easy.

When I got back to the living room, the guy was still in the kitchen, so I had a seat on the sofa and spread some sample magazines out on his coffee table. There was a picture on the end table of two people. I could tell one of them was him in his younger days. The hands gave it away. His arm was around someone with a beard. I was surprised to see this other person was a woman. A woman with a beard. They must have been part of a sideshow. I had always wondered if those beards were real.

He came back with two glasses. One in each claw.

"This woman in this picture with you," I said, "is that a real beard?"

At that he smiled. I knew that kind of smile. It was the kind Janine used to make when she'd talk about living with her grandmother for those couple years in the Adirondacks when she was a kid, or whenever someone would mention grandmothers, or the Adirondacks, or baklava, which she used to make with her grandmother in the Adirondacks.

"Ah, Francesca," he said, not saying whether or not the beard was real. But the way he said that, ah Francesca, she must have been the love of this guy's life. A lady with a beard. The truth is though, I can almost relate. Janine, she had a thin line of fuzz over her top lip. I think about that lip a lot. Sometimes I'd rub my tongue across that fuzz. It can be things that make someone different that make them appealing. It makes you feel like you have something special. Something no one else has. But I don't think I could handle a full beard.

He handed me a glass. "I hope you aren't offended if I have a drink," he said. "You could say I am a beer hobbyist, or maybe a beer exhibitionist," and he smiled a different kind of smile from the one before. I smiled back to be nice. "Everywhere in this world has something to offer me, but Belgians are the real kings of beer."

I drank some of my water. It was the kind with bubbles in it. Not what I expected, but I didn't mind it. "That Francesca," I said, "you guys married?"

"No," he said. "We used to travel the carnivals together."

"Carnivals," I said. "I wouldn't like all those people staring at me."

"People staring at you isn't a bad way to make a living," he said. "The ones to feel for were the ones like the fire-breathers. Nowadays things are different, but back then it would be a lot of kids picking up those kinds of tricks somewhere or another, on the street sometimes, trying to earn a living. The ones that didn't know what they were doing, their lips would bleed, and they'd have sores in their mouths and throats that wouldn't heal, because as you know, the show must go on. It always goes on. Those like myself, and the twins, and the Alligator Man, we had it easy. Most of all, I was lucky to be out there with someone like Francesca. Good company is the most important thing in life. Remember that." And there was that smile again.

I couldn't get over it. How he felt for her, this Francesca with a beard, after who knows how many years. Me, when I think about Janine, I am miserable. But that doesn't mean I can stop.

When I was packing my things from our apartment after she left, there was cat hair everywhere. Clumps of it in corners where I'd moved dressers, and all over. I used to hate that cat and all his hair. But I don't know, sweeping it all up, I didn't want to just dump it in the trash. I felt like I should do something with it. She loved that fucking cat. But what can you do with a bunch of cat hair, anyway? So I just left it in a pile in a corner.

She let me see her one time about a week or so after she left. Where we met, how long I could see her, everything had to be on her terms. It was like I was a child or a convict. So we met at a coffee shop a block away from her mother's house of all places. I don't even like coffee and she knows it. Anytime I'd try to touch her hand she'd pull it away. Do you know how that makes a guy feel? There was a time when we rearranged our whole lives for each other, and now I can't even touch her. What about everything we had before? What about how we used to stay up late drinking Old Style on the lawn in front of the apartment and talk about our future together? Our future. How someday we'd buy an old motel somewhere near the Adirondacks and fix it up ourselves, or maybe buy an RV and go from state to state selling baklava. Doesn't any of it count for anything now?

"Sure, there are those who put on a bit of an act for the crowd," he was still talking about the sideshow. "Marvin Bocott, who was billed as The Pinhead, had an unusually shaped skull. There was nothing wrong with his brain, but he played up to the crowd like he was something less than human. The crowd was always amazed at his ability to almost master simple actions. Like the way he could smoke a cigarette if someone in the audience would light it for him. If you want to know the truth, he was a quite skilled violinist."

I had nothing to add to this conversation. I drank the rest of my water and tried to listen to what he was telling me.

"It's about perception," he went on. "The crowd wants to see something unusual, maybe something unusually sad, and that sadness might loosen their pockets a little for the hard lives they perceive us to have, but mostly it makes them thankful that they have ten fingers and toes."

I'll admit, the idea of it sounds nice. Not having to kill yourself in a factory, or trying to convince people to buy some useless junk. Getting paid to just live. It sounds nice, but what good does that do a normal guy like me. Like I could gamble until someone cuts off my hands to settle a debt or something, and then I could try to convince Janine to get on steroids and maybe her fuzz would turn into a full beard. Then we could go on the road together in that RV and people might pay to watch me get drunk and pour myself shots with my feet. It's not an option for a regular guy like me.

I sat there in this guy's living room and couldn't stop thinking about Janine. I wanted to talk to her. I wanted to say something. "Do you got a phone I can use?" I said.

"Sure," he said. "It's in the kitchen next to the refrigerator."

But I didn't get up. I didn't know what I could say to her. I could tell her I was a month sober, but what would that matter? She would say something like, that's nice, or even, that she's proud of me. What more could I expect? That she'd take me back over it? It wouldn't change our past. I could tell her that I've changed. That I'd be good. That I wouldn't be the me that threw her pot of marigolds out the bedroom window. But if I really wanted to be honest with myself, I'd know it'd be a matter of time before things went back to how they were.

So I said to him, "Do you got any more of those Belgians?"

He went to the kitchen and came back with a fresh glass in each hand. "This beer," he said, "it's a style called gueuze. It's naturally fermented and quite sour. Almost like vinegar."

Even vinegar sounded fine to me. We sat and talked. He mostly talked. And we drank more beer. He told me more about the sideshow, and more about beer. I didn't sell him a magazine subscription, and he didn't tell me if that beard was real.

THE PUNCHING BAG

So I gave a punching bag to a kid with no arms. That makes me seem like a dick, I know. Let me back up a little.

"One more word, DiFranco. One more word." That's Coach Castillo. He's the instructor for this new alternative program at school. It's called Introducing Miracle Acres Students to Success in the Workforce, but to the rest of the school it's known as the In-My-Ass Program. The idea of it is to help teach the non-college bound, those of us who are either too lazy or too stupid to make anything out of ourselves, "the necessary skills to succeed in the real world," as Coach Castillo puts it. But I have my suspicions that the program was created to boost the county's dismal graduation numbers. What they teach us is a joke, but, me, I've never much cared for school, and in a program like this you don't really have things like homework and tests because the idea is to make it possible to get these fuckups across that stage come June.

So they want to teach us job skills. Truth is, to be fair, the only thing most of the dickwads in this program will need to know how to do is watch a conveyer belt or survive in prison. But, still, Coach had us spend a month on public speaking. As if one of these kids who will make it through high school barely able to read might one day give a presentation on the molecular structure of a peacock.

"Back straight. Quit playing pocket pool. Are you talking to us or are you daydreaming about getting a hummer in the janitor closet?" Coach would say. I don't know how many speeches about the legalization of marijuana I had to sit through. And not even ones with well-founded facts. And most of my idiot classmates would have slick smiles like they were being rebellious or original for talking about pot, and the others would give standing ovations. I am all for being rebellious, but what's the point if you are rebelling for something so common? It's like rebelling for out-of-the-closet masturbation.

So I gave a speech on how to make a crackpipe. "This is a car antenna," I said, making sure to sound enthusiastic but not too enthusiastic, making sure to keep constant eye contact with my audience, "just like you can find in any parking lot in America." I made a broad open gesture with my free hand. My classmates were rolling their eyes and sighing. "You'll only need a little piece. About four inches of the fat part." I heard someone, probably Jackie Sanders, who already popped out two babies by the time she was sixteen, mumble, 'Freakshow.' "For a filter I prefer using a little piece of a copper dish-scrubber. And I'd also recommend putting electrical tape on the end you will put your mouth on. These little guys get hot."

"That's enough, DiFranco," Coach said. "Real cute. Take your seat. Try pulling a stunt like that in a job interview and see where that takes you."

"I already have a job, Coach," I said, which was true. I wrote stories for one of those true confessions magazines. You know the kind. *I Was Forced Into Marriage at Age Thirteen. I'm a Man Who Was Raped By a Man.* The kind you can find on the lowest shelf of the magazine rack at your local grocery store. The kind that old ladies who look for reasons to believe the whole world is going to Hell read. Which is actually why I knew how to make a crackpipe in the first place. You can't make a deranged father burn his daughter with a crack pipe, a daughter who he keeps locked in the basement as a sex slave, convincing if you don't know what a crackpipe looks like. Okay, so I hadn't actually published a story in one of those magazines yet, but I was well acquainted with an editor for one, and he had been giving me encouraging feedback. He said I had the imagination for it. "I think my boss would be pleased by my well-roundedness."

"One more word, DiFranco. One more word."

Poor Coach Castillo. He got fired as the head football coach after another winless season, but they needed someone to run this new program, so they kept him on payroll. I imagine they thought having a natural disciplinarian would be good for a bunch of fuckups, or maybe they thought since he was a blue-collar guy he could relate to us better than most teachers. But if there's one reason Coach really could connect with these kids, it's because he's a failure too, even at what he loves. But he's not the kind of guy to admit that.

After word got out about all the time we spent in class talking about pot and crackpipes, Coach and the program took some heat from the administration. So his next big idea was to have us do some friendly community-service project.

"Everyone is saying they told you so," Coach said. "They told you you'd never amount to squat. Prove them wrong. This is your chance to make a difference."

"We could write a letter to some politician telling him to legalize weed," someone said.

"We could *all* write letters to the *President* telling him to legalize weed," someone else said.

Coach rubbed his balding head. This wasn't easy on him.

"Guys," I said. "He's talking about something like painting a mural at a daycare or something."

"Right. Yes. Good, DiFranco." Coach had a hopeful look on his face.

I couldn't help myself. "Something like Jesus and Satan giving each other a high-five underneath a rainbow, surrounded by babies and puppies."

"Goddamnit, DiFranco. One more word." Coach began rubbing his head again.

"Okay," I said. "Hear me out on this, Coach. It's true that no one expects anything out of us. But people expect even less out of the special ed. class."

"Beautiful insight," coach said. I thought he might rub the skin clean off his head. "Does anyone have a fucking idea or not?"

"No one gives a shit about those kids," I said. "I say we do something nice for them. Find out what each of them likes and give them a gift or something. Sign the gift, Anonymous, or The Happy Birthday Club. Something like that." Coach was at least paying attention "For example, Harry Phillips, I don't know what kind of disorder that dude has, but he is always flipping out and breaking things. Maybe we could give him a punching bag to take his aggression out on when he feels the need. Another example, Percy Sherman, that kid with no arms, he's my neighbor, I happen to know that he loves cartoons. He has posters up all over his room of Ren and Stimpy, dude even has like Mickey Mouse sheets, don't laugh. Sad part is his mother is always parked in front of the set watching soaps so he doesn't hardly get to watch anything. We could get him his own television. Doesn't have to be anything fancy. The smallest things can make a difference."

71

"Where would the money for these gifts come from, DiFranco?" Coach said.

"I was thinking maybe a sausage sale."

Okay, let me back up again. While it's true I hadn't actually published a story, I still had issues with the true confessions industry. It all followed a formula. What kind of an idiot can't follow a formula? Basically you could just retell the Cinderella story, but maybe replace the wicked stepmother with a sexually deranged friend of the family or a heroin addiction, replace the fairy godmother with a dude on a Harley with hair like John Stamos, he can replace the prince too by the way, and replace the ball with a beachside resort in Baja, Mexico. Then throw in some words like murderously and fate, and add a couple mentions of erect nipples, and bam, you have yourself a story.

But I wanted to put my stories on a different level. Inject some semblance of real life. Honest emotions. I grew tired of reading how the girl whose father impregnates her with a turkey baster, after daddy goes to jail and she visits the abortion clinic, goes on to lead perfectly normal teenage years, complete with a prom date with Mr. Niceguy-Football-Star. And I don't know how many stories I've read where a lady who is spousal-abused runs off with the charming, good-looking milkman or dogcatcher to live happily ever after. Real life, chances are that either A, she is going to come crawling back to Mr. Kidney-Puncher, or B, Mr. Milkman is also going to turn out to be some sort of creep. Let's face it, no one is going to want to read a story that includes several pages about years of therapy. And no one in the industry is going to write something entirely original, not that people want that either. But I'd like to give my stories a sense of honesty. So in real life, I want to see how people with difficult lives handle difficult situations. Hence giving a punching bag to a no-armed kid.

Okay, I still sound like a dick. Let me back up some more.

Percy Sherman and I have lived next door to each other in Miracle Acres' only housing project for about the last ten years. We have seen many single-mother families come and go through the years, but we have been a constant.

For my tenth birthday an uncle gave me a dachshund puppy. I named him Spiderman. No, I haven't always been this creative. I have seen Percy kick the poor little guy no less than a dozen times. And I imagine it is like cockroaches. If you see one, there is a hundred you don't see.

"What the fuck are you doing?" I said the first time I saw him kick Spiderman.

"Your dog took a shit in my yard," he said.

"No, he took a shit in the government's yard," I reminded him.

"If he does it again, I'll kick him again," he said.

"If you kick him again."

"Mom, the DiFranco boy is threatening me!" And before he ran inside, he said quiet enough so his mother wouldn't hear, "And your mother is a filthy tramp." Which I wouldn't have argued about even back then. My mother always has had plenty of guy friends staying over. I guess none of them liked her enough to move us out of these projects. But one of these guys was this magazine editor, so it's had its benefits once or twice.

As for the sausage sale, except for Jackie Sanders and Tom Walski abandoning their post to have sex behind the dumpster at K-Mart, which meant we were out the cost of their sausages, buns, and mustard, everything went as planned. We set up stands in front of local department stores and strip malls, and the class was enthusiastic enough since it was a Friday and we got to leave campus. Coach seemed proud of us. He even personally bought the first two gifts: a portable television and a heavy bag complete with a stand and bag gloves. When I volunteered to deliver the gifts, Coach took me aside and said, "We did all right today, DiFranco," and shook my hand.

What I had failed to consider during my planning and realized after I placed the wrapped box containing Harry Phillip's punching bag with a note saying "For Percy" on Percy's porch, was that on occasion Percy's dad comes around and picks him up. Sometimes he has him only for a couple hours and sometimes it's a couple days, but he's been coming around a bit more often lately as Percy's mom has been shedding a few of her extra chins.

So I sat around in the yard with Spiderman making the poor little guy listen to early drafts of the stories I was working on. But he mostly seemed disinterested and ate blades of grass from the few clumps that existed in our yard.

"Is it missing an erect-nipples reference, Spiderman? I am not going to do it, even if you think that's what it needs." He kept eating grass.

After a couple of hours Percy's mom came home, alone, and we watched as she waddled up the steps. She stopped and inspected the package, but after she realized the weight of the thing, she left it alone and waddled inside. And then it grew too dark for reading or revising, so I watched the glow from Percy's mom's television while Spiderman gnawed on one of my shoelaces.

Part of me felt truly sorry for Percy, and not just because of the no-arms thing, but because I wondered what the hell he did all day. I mean, I lived next door to him, and I didn't know of any hobbies the kid had. Me and him used to do some stuff together when we were younger. We'd walk down the train tracks till we got to the part that overlooked nice backyards. He loved it; he'd beg me to throw rocks into people's swimming pools. You should have heard the way he laughed when I sank them, like if you set a cat on fire or something, maybe the worst noise in the world, but I loved hearing it.

I can't tell you why I stopped hanging out with Percy, but it was before I ever saw him kick Spiderman. There are tons of things about myself that I don't have the answers for. I think this is part of my problem with the current state of true confession stories. Everyone is always discovering things about themselves. That their marriage is shit, or that they shouldn't be sleeping with their minister. I don't think any of us really understand ourselves very well.

On Saturday and Sunday, Spiderman and I hung out in the yard some more. I tried to read the stories as heartfelt sounding as possible, but it didn't raise his interest at all. "I'm serious," I told him, "the words *erect* and *nipple* will not appear next to each other in these stories." Though I got some good revising time in, Percy didn't show up while we were staking out his house.

On Monday after school I was putting Spiderman out on the chain and I looked over towards Percy's house. I could see through the cracks in the blinds that the punching bag was set up in a corner of his room. Waiting to be punched. Percy couldn't have set it up, and I can't imagine his mother would have done it. Maybe his father had done it when he brought him home.

Over the next few days I'd watch Percy through the blinds from my yard. Ant season was arriving in Miracle Acres and Spiderman's dish was being continually raided and it was becoming harder to concentrate on revising with the threat of hundreds of tiny teeth crawling up my socks. Sometimes Percy would lie on his bed and seem to stare at the bag. I don't know what he could have been thinking. And that bothered me. So I stopped watching.

One day I waited for Percy by the bus stop after school. The bus stop also doubles as the spot where old men from the neighborhood hang out and smoke. I usually try to avoid going anywhere near the bus stop so I don't get pulled into a conversation about the weather, or, and excuse my language, what these old men call young pussy. So I stayed about twenty feet back and avoided looking in the direction of the old men until I heard Percy's bus roll up. "Hey, Percy," I said as he got off the bus.

"Look, I haven't touched your dog," he said.

"It's not that," I said. "But thank you for that, I guess. Anyway, I was outside playing with Spiderman the other day, and I couldn't help but to see into your room. Is that a punching bag you have?"

"I don't know what you're talking about." He didn't even give me a suspicious look to see if I might have known where it came from.

"Yeah, I'm pretty sure that's what it was," I said. "A big, red heavy bag I think it's called. Maybe it says Everlast on it."

"Oh, that," he said. "What about it?"

"It's just that," I said, his eyes locked on mine, waiting for something. "Nothing. Never mind."

At class things had started to change. I'm not saying everyone had become saints or started planning a blood drive or anything, but there was definitely a noticeable shift in attitude. Some of the other students would spend their days volunteering at the special ed. class, playing games, finding out what the kids were interested in, and that sort of thing. Even Coach seemed to have more of a purpose and cursed less. He planned more sausage sales and talked about new locations we might want to target. He talked about saving money by doing online shopping whenever possible, and getting a class bank account. I even saw him reading a book on grant writing. Me, I had pretty much cleaned my hands with it all. I would show up to class and spend my days in the back of the room trying to avoid doing anything as much as possible. I hadn't even attempted to write a story in weeks.

Then one day Coach was quiet. No talk of sausage sales. Not one curse word. He told us to work on whatever we wanted. He spent the day with his dirty Nikes kicked up on his desk while reading copies of Sports Illustrated that were more than ten years old.

"Coach, I've been thinking that I could make personalized crackpipes for the entire special ed. program," I said to try to get something out of him.

Though this elicited groans from the rest of my classmates, Coach just said, "You do whatever you like, DiFranco."

When I was walking through the parking lot after school, I saw Coach standing near the football field, where he still parked every day, leaning on the fence and staring out at nothing. This was April so there wasn't even lines on the field. Maybe he was replaying all the losses in his head, or maybe he was trying to imagine a win.

"I saw you reading those magazines today," I said. "The Buffalo Bills going to the Super Bowl again. Big news, huh?"

Coach leaned back from the fence a little. I could see the muscles tighten in his forearms. He was a big guy but I didn't realize until just then that he still seemed to be in shape. Finally he let out a sigh and then said in a calm kind of way that I've never heard him speak, almost a whisper, "Look, they're pulling the plug on the program. They asked for my letter of resignation. Mrs. Jameson will finish out the year with you guys. You'll all still graduate." Mrs. Jameson was the school guidance counselor. She looked about ninety and acted even older. The kids in the program would eat her alive.

"But everything is going so well," I said. "Jackie Sanders has even been displaying the moral bearing of a nun."

He rubbed his bald head which looked like he had been up all night doing that. "Between you and me, DiFranco," he said. "Never mind. Fuck it. It doesn't matter. They honestly haven't told me much. But the school board is doing an investigation."

"Coach, if something happened, it wasn't your fault."

"Look at some of those kids, DiFranco. It all has to fall back on me. I should have my head checked for leaving anything up to some of those monsters."

"Some of those kids," I said, "you've made a difference."

"It's late in the fourth quarter. Thirty seconds left. You're down by ten, but you just forced a punt. You have the ball, but no real shot at winning the game. The right thing to do is take a knee. No reason to risk injury when the game is already over."

"What are you going to do?" I said, but felt like I should say more. Not that I had a confession in me, but Coach deserved something.

"I'll live, DiFranco." He took his hands off the fence and walked to his pickup truck. I followed him and he put a hand on the door handle. "I got an ex-wife," he said. "Me and her have been talking a little lately. Some years back there was things going on between us. Some things involving an illness. Bad times, you know. That had to do with why I came down here in the first place." He opened the door and got in the cab. "My wife, she said she'd be willing to see me. But I got a son too, well. Let's just say life is all about a series of starts. Remember that. We don't always get the endings we want, or some things maybe don't end at all, but we are always able to look forward to another start. "

I stupidly nodded my head like I could relate to what he was talking about.

"You're a smart kid," he said. "Do me a favor and start applying yourself. Good luck." And with that he closed the door, started the engine and drove out of the parking lot. I had to imagine he watched me through his rearview mirror standing alone watching him, still without anything to say, even to myself.

Justin Herrmann

HIGHWAY ONE, ANTARCTICA

I've never been to the North Pole or the South Pole, but I've been close. Polar-Circles close.

I was at a party at the carpenter shop my first month at McMurdo Station, Antarctica. There was always a party somewhere, but this one had a Journey cover band and a tyrannosaurus-shaped swing. Me and some other janitors listened to the band and shotgunned beers by the table saw. We'd been drinking for six hours straight and were still in our work Carhartts. There was a line at the shop's porta-john, so the four of us walked down the hill towards a dorm called Hotel California in the forty-below, the intensity of the midnight sun dulled by fifty-mile-an-hour sheets of gravel pelting our faces. We had keys to everything, so we detoured to the dorm boiler room to have another beer.

It was late October and the rest of the world seemed as far away as kindergarten. Not one of my coworkers had ever worked a day as a janitor before McMurdo. I just turned thirty and janitorial work was what I'd done for years. I never had less in common with a group of people, but I adored them anyway.

Ellen, who had a college degree in midwifery and a face like a Persian cat, said, "Christ, I can't have another sip or I'll pop. You're literally all in danger of urethra shrapnel."

Timothy, who was kind of motherly, said, "I don't think I could pee my pants even if I wanted."

Eddie, who had been a mailman, said, "I hate these pants."

"Someone come with me to the bathroom," Ellen said.

I punctured the bottom of a can of Speight's with my master key, then raised it to my mouth, pulled the tab and drank. I looked at the steel tread-plate floor. It was filthy with grease, but as rustless as a new toaster. Steam rose from the floor near Eddie, and a puddle formed around his shoes.

"It wasn't as hard as you'd think," Eddie said.

"Hell, I'm up for trying," Timothy said.

"Man, I want to pee with you guys too, just not in my pants. I have to walk home in these suckers," Ellen said. She stripped down to her underpants. Even down to her bra for some reason. She was as thin and shapeless as a barstool.

The idea was invigorating I thought. I had never used that word in my life. Invigorating. Then Ellen reached out and held my hand. Then I reached and held Timothy's hand. I couldn't go at first, then it came. The piss steamed from the floor all around us. Even Eddie went some more.

We stayed in that boiler room for a while in wet pants holding hands. Piss flowed along the steel tread into Ellen's pile of clothes.

I thought about all that for the first time in years today when I was changing my baby's diaper. She has colic bad, and a case of diaper rash that makes her look like she fell off the back of a Harley, so I held her tight against my chest and let her naked backside breathe. Sure enough, something I completely saw coming, a wet warmth spread down the front of my shirt. Her mother was asleep for what might've been the first time in days, so I was in no hurry to rustle something clean from the bedroom. Instead I walked out on my porch with the baby, still naked, still screaming, eyes focused on me like a gunfighter at high noon. All I could do was hold her tighter and stare into that toothless mouth and those tearless eyes. Thumb-shaped rhubarb sprouts were already pushing through the cool soil on the side of my house. My hands haven't touched that soil in a couple years, but the rhubarb comes back better each spring. I thought about that boiler room in Antarctica, and how after Ellen got dressed back into her pee-soaked clothes we all walked together to 155, the dorm we lived in. We stood together in 155's central hallway, Highway One, and shivered like wet cats. Ellen said "I'm going to love all you dudes forever. I mean that." Then Eddie said he meant that too.

LIGHTHOUSE

I was taken to a brothel a few times when I was thirteen and lived in a small town in Texas near the Mexican border. I had a friend, Bill Howard, whose dad was somehow or another involved in the Mexican radio industry and would meet business associates across the border at a place called Hunter's Ranch.

I'd heard a famous donkey show went on at Hunter's Ranch, but we'd go in the afternoon, and it looked like any bar I'd been to with my own dad. We never saw a donkey at Hunter's Ranch, just a couple hefty-armed women in skirts so tight it looked like they had packs of hot dogs taped to the back of their thighs.

Me and Bill would shoot pool and drink Cokes. Once one of the ladies walked over to the table me and Bill waited at. She stuck her fingers in my glass and fished out a Maraschino cherry. Then she chomped the cherry a few times before smiling at me and spitting the stem back into my glass. Sometimes Bill's dad would go behind a set of heavy doors with one of the women, and sometimes he wouldn't.

Eighteen years later I paid for sex for the first time at a brothel in Christchurch, New Zealand. My wife and I had separated, and my friend Julian, who's an artist and who spends time in Christchurch, recommended I go there to recover.

I didn't intend to go to brothels, though Julian recommended them too. I went to some bars. I had some drinks. I smiled at women. When they didn't smile back I had more drinks and watched old music videos on the television above the bar. Even when I was younger, before I was married, before I had a gut rising like pizza dough, before the hair on my chest was thicker than the hair on my head, I wasn't the kind of guy women would wait in line to go home with.

Julian told me to look for neon signs that read "Massage" with arrows pointing up unassuming stairwells above appliance stores and fish and chips joints. There wasn't a reason I chose one over any other except that it was on my way back to my hotel after striking out at the bar, or not even swinging would be a better stupid metaphor, and drinking always multiplies how sorry I feel for myself.

"Half hour or an hour," an unappealing-looking woman behind the counter asked, while I hoped she wasn't one of the prostitutes. The lobby reminded me of a doctor's office. Though it lacked an uncomfortable sofa—any sofa for that matter— and an outdated selection of magazines, the price seemed unreasonably high for the service provided, and with a door separating me from the prostitutes I suffered from nervousness.

"Half hour or an hour," the woman repeated.

I chose an hour because drinking also multiplies my faith in my abilities. I was led through a door into a room where four Maori women were sitting together on an antique-looking couch facing me. The room had red-wine-colored carpet, the uncomfortable-looking furniture the lobby lacked, and a pleasantness throughout that reminded me of my grandmother's house.

I visited a strip club a number of years back while passing through Nashville that had a sign that said "Hundreds of Beautiful Girls and Three Ugly Ones." It happened that the three ugly ones were the ones working that night in Nashville. It was honest and decent advertising that this brothel made no such claims about beauty. The women were old and heavy. There wasn't much to encourage me to pick one from another, so I picked the one who was wearing the most clothes.

She led me down a hall into a room that still reminded me of my grandmother's. My own house reminds me of my grandmother's too. My wife decorated it all with fake antique. Overpriced junk that was hard on my back to move. The stuff here looked real antique. Heavy stuff with red stain, a king-size with brass bed posts. There was a sticky sweetness about the place, and a shower in the corner with smooth tile, which she requested that I use to clean myself, specifically my genitals.

She was a big woman with a fat neck that engulfed her chin, and an overall shapelessness that reminded me of creatures that graze the bottom of the sea. But she was full of plenty of phony oohs and ahhs, and this I appreciated. My wife was thirty years old and never had an orgasm (not from sex anyway, she had one once during workouts for her aerobicise class). I'm not even sure she liked sex, but she could've put on a better show for my sake. It got to the point where I stopped ejaculating from sex too. On the occasions that we had sex, we were pointlessly rubbing our dry parts together. We're lucky we didn't burn down the house.

With this prostitute, our combined ugliness made me think of animals in the jungle.

I came back the next night. And I chose the same woman, but this time I paid for only a half hour. The night before I had finished well before the hour expired, but was only given the option to shower before I was directed to the entrance.

85

Even this time I finished before my time expired. I kept an eye on my wristwatch.

"You may clean yourself in the shower if you wish," she said.

"I have twelve minutes left," I said.

"Excuse me."

"It's twelve forty-four. I should get the time I paid for."

"You've had your pop. That's how it works. What do you think? You don't complain when your pictures are developed in less than an hour, do you? If you want more, you can pay for more." She looked at my genitals. "Could you even get it up again?"

I would have to admit it would be a challenge in the time remaining. "How about we talk?"

"What is there to talk about?" She stood, and I watched as she slid her underpants back on.

"Do you ever orgasm?"

"Look, if you want me to talk dirty, you're going to have to pay."

"I'm sorry. I mean it as a serious question."

"From a customer?"

"Yes."

"No."

"Why not?"

"There is no passion or desire in this."

"Can't you fool yourself?" I can't say I liked looking at her body in the traditional sense, but there was a kind of beauty there, like a nice sofa or a lighthouse.

"Why would I want to? And your time is up."

"I would like to talk some more."

"We can do what you like, but it all costs the same."

"No, I mean, maybe over coffee. I don't know anyone here. I thought maybe you'd be interested in meeting after work."

"I don't give freebies either if that's what you're after. But I like to eat after work. You may meet me at a place called The Honey Pot on the corner of Lichfield and Manchester at four thirty."

I met her at the Honey Pot. She ate with a ferocious appetite, but who knows, in her line of work she may burn as many calories as an Olympic swimmer. I learned her name was Alana and I began meeting her every night she worked for sex and every morning after for a meal. We talked about all sorts of things, most of them of no value other than to reinforce a human companionship, but she told me why and how she got into the prostitution business, which I'll respect her by not sharing, but I'll say the reasoning didn't make much sense to me, though I'll also say what I've told her about my marriage didn't make much sense to her.

I'd sleep for twelve hours a day so I'd have to occupy less time in between these meetings. Before I arrived in New Zealand, Julian told me all sorts of things to do, walk barefoot in the fine sand and cool waters of Golden Bay, kayak with the dolphins in the fjordlands, bathe in the hot pools at Franz Josef Glacier. The problem with nature, while it may offer lots of ways to please the senses, it does little to distract the mind. Nothing mends a broken heart like sex and companionship, even when you have to pay for it.

On some mornings a coworker of Alana's, Tina, would join us for food. She was a large sad woman who was missing all of her front teeth. When she yelled, which was most of the time, her loose jowls made me think of a talking basset hound. She had discovered that her oldest daughter started working at a brothel.

"I will die before I allow the little bitch to live this way," she said. "I have sacrificed too much. A couple nights ago I went there and carried her out like a child. She was screaming and clawing at my face, and she bit my shoulder until she drew blood. Customers will see that mark on my body and try it themselves. It is bad for business. She went back last night so I followed her. When they saw me come in, three of the other girls forced me back down the stairs by hitting at me with their shoes. I went home and grabbed the first thing I could find with some weight to it, and then I went back to that whorehouse and smashed their window out with my iron. Understand she is my baby."

"Tina, honey," Alana said. Then Tina started crying and Alana said again, "Tina, honey."

I didn't like Tina joining us. To hell with her and her problems. It made me think of my own problems.

One night while I was in bed with Alana I heard some commotion out in the hallway. I was initially alarmed because brothels should be peaceful places by nature, but I thought to myself, to hell with that commotion, it makes me think of my own past commotions.

A moment later I heard the door open. A blonde woman entered the room. She was tall and attractive so I knew she didn't belong. She was holding a large black club like the ones the police carry, but I have never seen a police officer that looked like that.

"What the hell is going on?" I said to the woman.

She was not interested in small talk. Instead of answering my question, she attempted to strike at me with the club, but I rolled off the bed and the blow instead struck poor Alana's face.

I stood and faced the beautiful villain. She had no way of knowing I was a black belt in judo. I was good. I once placed second in Junior Nationals, but I hadn't competed in years. It was one of the things I gave up for my marriage.

"Honestly, grown men kicking and punching at each other," my wife had said early in our marriage.

"Baby, it's judo. There's no punching or kicking. Just grappling. If you'd come watch sometime,"

"If I wanted to watch men 'grapple,' it wouldn't be you and your friends. It would be on a stage in Vegas."

What could I say to that? So I said nothing.

"Why don't you use all that extra testosterone to do something useful like build us a deck or fix all the leaky faucets in this piece-of-shit house?"

For one thing it's because I had never built or fixed anything in my entire life. It's funny how that sort of thing works. My hands are capable of applying perfect single-wing or ezekiel chokes, but worthless when holding a screwdriver or wrench. They aren't transferable skills.

I gave up judo, but never got those fucking faucets to stop leaking.

And though I hadn't practiced judo in years, it all came back the moment the beautiful villain swung her club at me again. I stepped forward and caught her arm just below the elbow and wrapped my other arm around her waist and executed a near-perfect *harai goshi* and tossed her flat on her back. It was a beautiful throw. It would have received many oohs and ahhs from an audience in competition, but wouldn't have scored a full point; I had been surprised by her lightness which caused me to lose my balance and fall to the ground as well, but this put me in a good position to apply a *kesa gatame*, a pinning technique. I have never struck a woman in my life, and wasn't going to start, but in this position I would have the chance to reason with her and discover the meaning of her attack.

"What the fuck are you doing?" I said.

She said nothing.

"I swear to god, I will strangle you with your own arm if you don't start talking." I lied.

"Okay, okay. No reason to do anything rash."

"Says the woman who hits people with clubs."

"Yes, that is the nature of war, my friend. We came here to pay these bitches back. One of these used-up whores has been upsetting our business lately."

A war between brothels. It made me wonder how things would have gone had I happened upon this other brothel first. Would this beautiful prostitute have joined me every morning for breakfast? If she had, would I have stupidly fallen in love?

I didn't like the feeling of violence coupled with my nakedness. I was about to loosen my hold on this woman so I could check on my friend Alana, take her to the hospital if need be, but then another couple of fit-looking women came into the room. They were also armed with clubs and began beating me. I was being hit from all angles with clubs and shoes with pointed toes and tiny fists. I did my best to cover up, but I felt a warmth begin to envelope my head and a ringing in my ears. I felt weightless and wet as if underwater.

I awoke in the familiar bed I spent many half-hour increments in. Alana was sitting on the edge of the bed holding a sponge. I imagined she had been washing blood from my skin. She herself had a bandage above her eyebrow that went to her hairline.

"It is good to see your eyes open," she said. "We will not be taking any more customers tonight."

"I'll get dressed," I said.

"No, you are fine here. You were never able to finish earlier. I owe you if you are feeling up to it."

With the pounding I felt in my head, I couldn't tell if sex would make it better or worse, but I told her I wasn't up to it. I could tell in her eyes my decision made no difference to her. I was surprised to discover that I was disappointed that she wasn't disappointed.

"Well, maybe you can cash it in some other time. There is always tomorrow."

"I've been thinking that tomorrow I may take my friend Julian's advice and check out Golden Bay." This was a lie. I hadn't been thinking that at all. It just came to me as I said it. But still, it sounded like something I might like to do.

"The saltwater will be good for your wounds."

"Thank you," I said. "I should go."

"Not yet," she said. "Let me finish what I have started," and she leaned in and began rubbing the sponge on my face.

My Last Name Is Hitler

I had asked my father if we were related to Adolf Hitler, and he said that we weren't. I asked my Uncle Lou the same question, and he said that we weren't. I asked my grandfather, and he said to quit worrying about a name. He said, "If you're an asshole, people are going to think you're an asshole regardless of your name. If you're a good person, if you do good things, if you're the kind of person that says 'it's not a favor if you have to pay for it' and avoid stepping on ants, people won't give a shit about a thing like a name." It's too bad my grandfather is dead now.

My grandfather never had to go to war because one of his hands was mutilated in an accident at a steel mill. After World War II he earned a living drawing caricatures at state fairs and carnivals. He said people love spending money on looking at themselves when times are good. Even though his dominant hand was crushed, he was still able to draw beautifully. He said you draw with your mind, not your hands. I draw as well, but I am not sure I agree with him. If I trusted my mind over my hands and eyes, I'd be in danger of becoming a pornographer. This wouldn't have bothered my grandfather.

It isn't easy getting a job when your last name is Hitler. My father and uncle own their own company, perhaps due to this problem. I could work for them. They've asked me. They value my delicate hands. But I don't want to work for them. They are also artists of sorts. They handcraft ceramic dildos. They are the best on the market. Praised for their strength. Perhaps you are thinking I don't want to work for them because I have moral objections. That is not the case. I have sexual objections. I fear the time I have spent around these dildos has desensitized me from sex. Not that I've had many chances, in fact I've only had one, but it's not the kind of thing I want to risk.

At the places I've applied for work, I believe my application gets thrown out because they think it's a joke or something. I'm sure of it. Here's how it goes. I walk into the grocery store, or whatever, where I turned my application in weeks ago. I go up to the service desk. "Excuse me, sir," I ask. "I applied here a couple weeks ago and I was wondering if you guys were hiring yet?"

"What's your last name? I'll look up your application," they say.

I hesitate. "Hitler," I say.

They pause for a moment while my response replays in their head to make sure they heard me right. "Hitler? Nope, not seeing your application. Definitely no Hitlers. You can fill out another application if you like, Mr. Hitler."

Why do I need to fill out another one? I have already filled one out. "Isn't there a manager or someone I can talk to instead?"

So they call up to the manager's office. "Sir, there is a Mr. Hitler here who would like to talk to you, if you have a moment, Sir."

"Tell Hitler that I'm on the other line with 'ol Joe Stalin," the manager likely replies.

"No sir, it's a guy here. He wants a job."

At this point, if the manager bothers to come down, he might shake my hand. "Last name's Hitler, eh?" They look me over real good to see if I am doing this for a prank or something, glance around to see if there others who may have put me up to this peeking around the corner of the toothpaste and contraceptives aisle. If they decide I might be serious, they'll ask me why I want to work at their store.

"I just want a job," I say, maybe a little too forcefully.

Then the manager decides I have an attitude problem and tells me to fill out another application. He thanks me for my time and assures me that he'll keep me in mind when they are next hiring.

Maybe I do have an attitude problem. Yeah, I get it. I have the last name in common with a really bad guy. Trust me though; give me this job and these hands will only touch groceries. They won't kill a single Jew. I swear.

I had a girlfriend once. Well, there was this girl, and I went out with her a few times. Her name was Heidi Goldstein, but she went by the name Edna St. Vincent after her favorite poet. She hung out with an artsy crowd and smoked long cigarettes and drank merlot; too much merlot. She was a drunk. She was the kind of girl who didn't like petting puppies. Her hips were too wide and her mouth was disproportionately big for her face and she talked about things I didn't care about. "It's the collective ignorance of the American people that allows our government to exploit third world nations and capitalize off their slave labor … politicians … corporate interest … freedom. Are you even listening to me?"

We met at a drawing class offered at the university. She told me that I was great at drawing, perhaps the best in class, but I could never be a real artist because I had no imagination.

"I mean, sure," she said, "you can draw a pony, and it will be a really fine-looking pony, but who the hell wants to look at a picture of a pony. And, yeah, maybe you could give the picture to some seven-year-old girl, and maybe she would kind of like it for a day, but then she'll just stuff it in her closet when her creepy Uncle Eddie brings her a velvet poster of a pink unicorn rising tall in a field of silver daisies in front of a magnificent seven-colored rainbow."

"Rainbow?" I said.

"Magnificent seven-colored rainbow," she said.

"What about your picture of the little girl picking wildflowers? That was simple but nice. She had those socks with pictures of kittens on them," I said.

"You don't get it, Richard Hitler." She liked saying my first and last names together. "That is supposed to be a sad picture," she said. "Tragic. The joy and carelessness she feels now will be taken, ripped from her. All the problems that harden the female soul stand before her: abusive relationships, inequality, et cetera, et cetera. Her innocence will be stolen."

"I like her socks," I said.

She shared an apartment with a musician named Sven. At least she said he was a musician. I never actually saw him playing an instrument, or heard of him playing anywhere. In fact, I never saw him do much of anything besides smoke and eat Cheetos. And he wasn't even good at that. He always had crumbs in his beard and his cigarettes would burn down to the filter while he stared off at a lamp or door handle. Edna said he was deep. He said that he read Adolf Hitler was in love with his own mother. He asked if I wanted to fuck my mother too. Edna laughed.

Edna and I tried to have sex once, but I couldn't get an erection.

"What's wrong with it?" she said.

"I don't know. I think I am too nervous," I said. I had masturbated while thinking about her dozens of times. In fact, I had masturbated while thinking of her earlier that day.

"Oh," she said. "Well, let's drink some more."

I didn't see her much after that.

In junior high, it was a common insult among girls to say that someone was going to marry me. "You're going to be the next Mrs. Hitler and have a bunch of little Hitler babies." I masturbated to many of those girls too.

Adolph Hitler was denied admission to the Vienna Academy of Fine Arts. Twice. He was eighteen when he was first rejected. His test drawings were unsatisfactory. The second time he was rejected on the grounds that his art exhibited more architectural skill than artistic. He struggled for a while trying to earn a living as an artist. He sold his paintings on the street. As a boy, he was told that he lacked the necessary funds and personal contacts to be a successful artist. I've seen his artwork. It's not bad. He painted a lot of pretty landscapes. Churches too. Lots of churches. He painted well-known city views of Vienna. I imagine these were the easiest to sell.

It seems a lot more respectable to recreate a thing as it is, rather than to create something new altogether. Such precise skill is required to illustrate every exact detail of something real. A lot of this concept art seems like a scam. Great, Edna, there's a painting of an armless man in a funhouse, burning a baby with a cigarette between his toes, as a bearded woman holds down the child and a single tear runs down her cheek. What the hell does that mean? How can you admire what you can't understand?

In class we learned about Piss Christ. This guy Serrano puts a crucifix in a jar of piss, and some people are outraged about it. Artists lose funding. But the value of Serrano's own work rises. All for putting a crucifix in piss.

One day a few weeks back I was a little depressed about not having any luck with employment. I was at a dumpy coffee house drinking a boysenberry-rice-milk latte, something I normally wouldn't have, but I was following up on an application so I figured I should order a drink. The place had bad local artwork on the walls with high price tags.

I went home and created a piece I would call "Mother Mary Sucking Off the Pope: Crayons and Markers on Construction Paper Number Seven." As the title suggests, I used crayons and markers as my tools instead of watercolors and brushes (I didn't really use construction paper, I used poster board, but I liked the way construction paper sounded in the title). The Pope sits in a large throne, mostly purple marker. His outfit is white with yellowy-orange-if-not-quite-golden trim (I choose to use the traditional Crayola eight-pack instead of the more practical sixty-four). His face is old and contorted, red crayon, very faint, giving him a pinkish complexion, but perversely smiling. A woman in a Crayola-blue dress and brown sandals kneels face down in the Pope's lap. Her long brown hair is in a red shawl. A magnificent seven-colored rainbow shines behind them.

It took less than two hours to complete and I brought it to the coffee house that wouldn't give me a job. It was a place Edna had taken me before, a place, according to Edna, full of poets who weren't very good musicians and musicians who weren't very good poets.

The manager of the place was happy enough to display my work, and despite the fact that he wouldn't give me a job before, upon seeing my work, acted like we were friends. He had a Master's Degree in philosophy and the hair creeping up from the front of his shirt collar was longer than the hair on top of his head. He told me he did what he could to support the local scene, and he knows all too well what a struggle it is out there in this day and age for an artist, so if there was anything he could do to help me out, he'd be glad to. I thought about asking him again for a job, but I feared that kind of forwardness would make me sound like less of an artist, so I ordered another boysenberry-rice-milk latte.

I once watched a show on TV about Adolf Hitler. The show claimed that during his public speeches, he would get so worked up that he would often ejaculate, right there in his pants, right there while giving his speeches. I wonder if he was that passionate about his art. He is estimated to have produced as many as three thousand pieces of art in his lifetime. The show also said that he was addicted to methamphetamines during World War II. The quality of his artwork noticeably declined over the years. I wonder if that is connected with his possible drug addiction. Or maybe he lost his passion. Or maybe he just didn't have time.

Only a few days passed before I heard anything about my drawing. I received a call from a gentleman interested in purchasing it. He wanted to meet me in person. His name was Andrew. He said to meet at the coffee shop where my picture was displayed. He told me he would be sitting at the table directly under my picture.

"Mr. Hitler," he said as I approached the table. He stood and shook my hand. "It is a great pleasure to meet you." He was a small old man whose cheeks drooped as if they were made out of soft clay, and he had a warm grandfatherly smile, not like my grandfather, but one like you'd want a grandfather to have. There was a young lady in the chair next to him. She could have been twelve or twenty, it was hard to tell, but she was much better-looking than Edna and she had these eyes that were easily four shades lighter than Crayola's standard blue that seemed to be fixed on me. "Please, have a seat, young man," Andrew said. He had a gentle way about speaking, like if an oak tree could talk.

"Thank you," I said. I seated myself across from them at the table.

"This is my granddaughter, Sadie. She likes to draw too. It's all about passion, isn't it?"

"Passion," I said. "Yes, it is."

"I have a small church that I preach at, and Sadie helps me out quite a bit there. Your work will fit in nicely."

I worried that they misunderstood what I intended the piece to mean. Maybe he didn't look at the title and thought Mother Mary was just embracing the Pope. I didn't imagine it would be fitting for a church, but then again my grandfather always said that the meaning a viewer gives a piece is more important than the meaning the artist intended. "Great," I said. "I hope your congregation enjoys it."

The manager came to our table and asked what he could get for us. He told me he was glad to see me back. Andrew ordered two coffees, black, and three chocolate cupcakes. I ordered a strawberry pop this time.

"Andrew," I said, "do you come here often?"

"I do," he said. "I try to frequent as many places anymore as my old body can stomach." The pleasant smile remained on his face. I smiled back.

"That's nice," I said. "Do you look for people to recruit for your church?"

"No," he said, "I look for things to talk about at church."

The manager came to our table with our drinks and the cupcakes. Andrew placed a cupcake in front of Sadie and kept two in front of himself.

I looked at Sadie who was still looking at me. She took a bite of her cupcake and chocolate stuck to her teeth. That would have bothered me if it happened to Edna, like when her teeth would be stained red from Carlo Rossi. But chocolate teeth was an adorable look on Sadie.

"'Thou shall not make unto thee any graven image, or any likeness of anything that is in the heaven above, or that is in the earth beneath, or that is in the water beneath the earth. Thou shall not bow down thyself to them.' What verse is that, Sadie?" Andrew said.

"Exodus twenty four," she said without hesitation.

"Very good, Pumpkin," he said.

I felt Sadie's foot rub against mine. It is a little thing, but it gave me an erection nonetheless. It's odd how things seem to work when you don't need them to.

"Sinning is as commonplace in this country as sneezing," Andrew said. "Pumpkin, what do you think of this cupcake? Moist, no? They do good here. They add a half cup of mayonnaise to their batter. The oils in it keep it moist. Wonderful. The open homosexuality in this country influences the youth."

I was admiring the springy-looking texture of Andrew's cupcake, then I said "Homosexuality?"

I think he thought I said "homosexuality" to reiterate his point because then he leaned his face close enough to mine so that I could smell the chocolate on his breath. "I have seen two men kissing in this very establishment, and no one gives it a second thought," he said. Then he leaned back in his chair and looked down at his cupcake. "And further, mayonnaise contains vinegar which will help preserve the texture of the cupcake for days." He dug his fork prongs down into the cupcake, and the cake was wet enough that I could hear it squish as the fork pushed through and then he lifted a heaping bite to his mouth. Then he said between chews, "'If a man lies with a man as he would with a woman, both have committed an abomination. They shall be put to death. Their blood is upon them.' Sadie?"

"Leviticus twenty thirteen."

"Death?" I said, this time a bit more shocked, and I don't know if he thought I was reiterating his point again, or if he was chewing that cupcake too loud to hear me, or maybe I don't have enough conversations to realize how I sound, or maybe I didn't actually say anything.

Sadie's foot was now rubbing my leg. I grew even harder.

"Everything is spelled out for us. Listen, Sadie, I believe they use beet powder to get this slight purple tint in the cake. I think I can taste it." Sweat was beading up on his wrinkled forehead.

Sadie's foot went higher, now above my kneecap. I began to think there was the threat of ejaculating in my pants as Adolf had.

"The evils and dangers of this nation must be recognized." He forked the last portion of the cupcake into his mouth. "Mr. Hitler, tell me if you taste the beet powder?" He wiped the sweat from his forehead with his sleeve and offered me the other cupcake.

Just then Sadie's foot made its way near my groin and I did ejaculate. Right there in my pants, right there while sitting across from this man and his misguided yet beautiful granddaughter. It's the way it goes that your brain becomes clear once you ejaculate, and I thought for a moment. I thought about my favorite of Adolf's paintings, a watercolor of the Karls Church in Vienna. It's wintertime; a very grey portrait. There are a handful of people walking and a couple of horses and carriages in the snow-covered road in front of the church. Just a moment in time in life.

And I looked at Sadie, her eyes still fixed on me, and I thought she was maybe still young enough to still like pictures of ponies. And I thought that I would like to go home and start a new picture. Maybe I'd give oil painting a try, and maybe pretty landscapes.

Then I said to Sadie, "Do you like ponies?"

She turned and looked at her grandfather with what I thought may have been a look of hope. She turned back and shook her head.

So I stood up and went to the picture of the Pope, and tore the bottom right corner off of it where I had signed my name. I took the picture off the wall and set it on the table in front of Andrew. "It's yours," I said. I took two dollar bills out of my pocket and set them on the table to cover the cost of my pop.

As I walked towards the door, I heard Sadie say to her grandfather, "Leviticus twenty thirteen."

THE NEW CITY HOTEL

I was in Christchurch, New Zealand after spending six months at a place called McMurdo in Antarctica working as a carpenter. In a few days an earthquake would devastate Christchurch, but when I walked through Cathedral Square and Hagley Park, along the Avon River and Oxford Terrace, as beautiful as it was, all my mind was capable of was wondering about my girlfriend Emily back home in Rockford who was pregnant by some Guatemalan guy who did dishes at the restaurant she worked at.

The weather was welcoming that first day in Christchurch. And by welcoming, I mean it was damp and gray. There was substance to the air, something you could feel. Believe me, any change is a blessing after sixth months of sunshine. I was put up in a hip eighty-dollar-a-night hotel on Cashel Street. The kind of place I'd only stay if someone else was paying the bill. It was close to plenty of restaurants, cafes, and dance clubs, none of which were the kind of places I felt like going to. So I went for a walk up Colombo Street looking for a bar. Somewhere to have a drink where no one could order an Asian papaya salad or a cranberry-infused Mojito.

Ten or so blocks and I was in a part of town where the friendly cafés had turned into garages, and the Thai restaurants into empty windows and vacant lots. The only retail store on the block was a canary-yellow building named The Baby Factory, and I was surprised to see that it was actually a store that sold baby products,. I thought about going in and looking for onesies with pictures of the kiwi bird or something like that, but I changed my mind when I saw what I'd been looking for across the street. There was a three-story water-stained building with a wraparound balcony that looked like it could crumble at any moment. Fading letters were painted near the top of the building that read "The New City Hotel," and above the entrance an equally faded, hand-painted sign read, "Tavern."

The inside of the bar was large and mostly empty of furniture except for a couple heavy looking wooden tables, most likely oak, unoccupied, placed around the room with no sense of order. Nothing on the walls, except faded paint and exposed plaster, that linked it to its past, to the years when the New City Hotel and this neighborhood might have been part of the life of the city. Sometimes things change for the better, and sometimes they don't. This was the kind of dump I met Emily in a few years back, and I can't say I wouldn't have liked to meet someone like her there, or anyone for that matter, love or not, someone to make me forget about Emily and that baby of hers for a while. But I was out of luck because the only other customers were a bony Maori woman with a face like a bulldog, and sitting next to her was a skinny guy who had an unhealthy look about him. They both were drinking beer by the pitcher.

I brought a girl back to my room in Antarctica a couple times. A heavyset girl who worked in the kitchen. She had the reputation for having been around. If there's one thing I know about girls like that, it's that they have their own troubles. But

I didn't care to know the first thing about her troubles. And I didn't care to tell her about myself. In the mornings, when I'd sobered up, I'd only proven to myself that I could still screw fat girls. It made me miss Emily even more.

Emily and I had one of those relationships where one of us was always leaving the other. Things would be fine one minute, and then the next I'd spit at her or she'd hit me with the vacuum cleaner. It went on like that.

I'd go to the bar every night like clockwork at McMurdo, and I'd call Emily on those nights I missed her most.

"I love you," I'd always say.

"I'm pregnant," she said one time.

"Me and you, we've been through some things," I said.

"It's not yours," she said.

At that point, despite what she had just said, I felt I needed her so much she could have told me she had poisonous skin and it wouldn't have bothered me. Though maybe poisonous skin would seem more reasonable than pregnancy to some. So I told her whatever I could, like I had many times before, to keep her from leaving me for good, things I probably believed every word of at the time.

The bartender at the New City Hotel was a toothless guy with a neck like a tractor tire. The bar itself was hand-carved cherry wood. The kind of work you could break a beer bottle on and not even scratch. I sat a couple stools down from the others and ordered a Speight's and a double Southern, not something I normally drank, but I felt like something different. I could tell by the way that the three of them looked at me that they didn't get many Americans here this far down Colombo Street. I knocked back the Southern and the sweetness made me clench my teeth. But I ordered another. Then another. I had money to spend there, so I felt like I should.

"What part of America are you from, sweetie?" the woman asked me.

"I'm not from any part," I said. Then, though I felt the statement was mostly true, I thought it made me sound standoffish, something I normally try to avoid, so I added, "The middle part. Near Chicago."

"Illinois, right?" the unhealthy-looking guy said, and he ended Illinois with an S, though it didn't bother me like it would most people from Illinois, because, as I said, I am not really from anywhere. "The name is Mickey," the guy went on. "And this is my friend Melanie, though sometimes she prefers the name Stephanie. She's a fifty-six-year-old bipolar schizophrenic. She's crazy as a fucking monkey on the speed. Ain't that right, Melanie? Aren't you fucking crazy?"

"My name is Stephanie," she said to me, and looked me in the eye. She seemed sure of who she was, which is more than I can say about myself most of the time.

Mickey stood up from his stool and sat in the spot next to me with his pitcher. He topped off my glass of Speight's. "So, you here on holiday, are you, mate?" he said.

"Yeah," I said. "Holiday."

Me and Emily used to sit in the tub of the apartment she had because the shower never worked, and we'd talk about the places we'd eventually go together. We'd sit there sometimes for hours drinking Pabst, or champagne, or bourbon. Sometimes we'd talk about Japan, and sometimes we'd talk about Arizona. It could have been anywhere. I used to rub her body with lotion after the baths in those good days.

But that was back then. Before we started fighting. Before she cut my hand open with a steak knife and took me to the hospital where I got fourteen stitches, all for what I don't even remember.

"That's good," Mickey said. "Holidays. The world is yours to enjoy. Cheers," he said, and raised his glass to me.

"Cheers," I said back, and put money on the bar for another round.

"Do you get high, mate?" Mickey said. "Me and Melanie, we're going upstairs in a few to have a smoke if you care to join us."

The truth is, I've never much cared for marijuana, but I always try to make it a habit not to turn down the generosity of strangers, so I said, "Sounds good."

We finished our drinks and then I followed them through a door in the back of the bar that led to a damp stairwell that smelled of bleach and popcorn. Upstairs there was a red-carpeted hallway lined with a half-dozen or so doors on each side. Melanie or Stephanie used a key to open one of the rooms. Inside the apartment one of the walls was almost completely covered with wooden crucifixes and paintings of Jesus Christ. There must have been fifteen or more of various sizes. A wall of Jesus Christs.

"Please, have a seat right here," she said and motioned for me to sit on a couch that faced the Christs. Mickey sat next to me on the couch and she sat in a pine rocking chair that faced us. "I don't feel like looking at our Lord and Savior when I am smoking marijuana," she said.

Mickey took a plastic bag and some rolling papers from his shirt pocket. He rolled a joint as fat as my thumb. He handed it to me along with a lighter. I lit the joint and took a couple hits. I felt a burn in my lungs I hadn't felt in a long time. It made me feel like a me from years ago, a me that still got excited about all kinds of things, like hanging dry wall and learning to use a table saw. Then I passed it across to Melanie.

"What kind of work do you do back in America?" Mickey said to me.

"I build things mostly," I said. "Roofs, sundecks, toy horses. You name it. You?" I said to Mickey.

"Mickey," Melanie said, "he don't do nothing."

I didn't know if these two were a couple, or just friends. But everything that was said between them, you could tell the other took lightly. The looks Emily gave me could freeze vodka.

"I want to get diving equipment," Mickey said. "The professional stuff. And I want to get a boat and explore the ocean. Like Jacques Cousteau. It's my dream. Been my dream forever. Hunt for sunken treasure and all. Maybe take tourists. Take them out diving. Take them looking for treasure."

"That's some dream. Good luck with that," I said, and I meant it.

We finished smoking that joint and Mickey rolled another one. I was already high, but I kept going because it was offered. I've always been like that.

"Do you have a girlfriend?" Melanie said to me.

"No," I said. "I mean yes." Then, and I don't know what made me do it, maybe it was the marijuana and the booze, or maybe it was something else, but I started telling those strangers about Emily. I told them the same sort of things that I've been telling you. About the Guatemalan dishwasher and the baby. I told them about the baths and about Japan. I told them about Antarctica and the fat girl, and about how I would like to hear that Emily had an abortion or miscarriage so that we could go on like we had before. And I told them that I couldn't blame her for finding someone else, that it didn't take much to make someone better than me, that I've done some things, and she's done some things, so the best thing for the both of us might be to let her go, but things like that are never easy, and I don't have the strength for it anyway.

Then no one said anything else for a while. Mickey shook his head and rolled another joint, and Melanie turned and faced her wall of Jesus Christs.

When she turned back towards me, I was worried that she was going to tell me something about Jesus having a plan for me, but instead she said, "I have five fingers." Then she said again, "I have five fingers. Just like you," and held up her hand, palm out, fingers spread wide for me to see.

I nodded like I understood, but I didn't know what she was trying to tell me. Maybe she was offering me a handjob. She might have been a prostitute in her better days, or still is. Not that I'd judge her or anyone else for that. Or maybe she wanted me to see that I don't need a woman to be happy in this world. Or maybe she wanted me to see something about humanity, something that I couldn't see.

We sat there a while longer without much being said. We passed around that joint, and I studied the Jesus Christs. It surprised me how similar the Christs looked to each other even though they must have been painted by different artists. Like people are certain what the guy looked like, as if they are painting portraits of Elvis or something. We sat there smoking, and I enjoyed the company.

When I left The New City Hotel I was surprised to see that it had started raining. I hadn't seen rain for six months. The first time you see something like that again it seems unreal. There was a young woman across the street pushing a stroller over the tiny cracks in the sidewalk. There was a hood over the stroller that was probably keeping the baby dry, but this woman, she was soaking wet. Her T-shirt was pressed tight against her skin, and

I could make out the lines of her bra. The wetness from the rain made her mascara run making it look as if she'd been crying.

When me and Emily first got together, before the spitting and knives, before we began falling asleep with our clothes on, when I felt lucky to have a girl like that, we had walked to a carnival together in the rain. It was really coming down. The rides were all closed, of course, but some of the carnies were still around, trying to wait the weather out because it was still early. Some of the food stands were still open, and we fed each other corndogs and funnel cakes along with Vicodin and a pint of bourbon we brought. And I traded a few Vicodin for a stuffed rhinoceros for Emily from a guy at the ring-toss stand. The rain wasn't letting up, and me, her and the rhino were soaked. We ended up ducking into a porta-potty and felt each other up and kissed. We must have went at it like that for twenty minutes. Her mascara was running and I told her how pretty she looked like that. I would see her mascara run more times than I'd care to count over the next few years. But that night I told her there was no one else in the world like her. After that a lot of things happened between us. People have told her things about me, and me things about her. But it was no one else's situation to judge then, and it's not their situation to judge now. Even I don't know what the hell to think. But I know it's not a matter of wanting or not wanting. I know that much.

I watched that young woman push that stroller in the rain. I crossed the street and followed her. She turned down a side a street and headed away from the heart of the city. I followed her over sidewalks that were already severely cracked and broken, past vacant lots and into a neighborhood full of single-story brick houses that weren't spectacular, but they mostly had nice lawns. I caught up with the woman and looked down at the baby as I passed. The baby was awake and he looked up at me with these blue eyes. I said, "That's a good-looking baby you have, miss." Though truthfully it looked like any average baby.

I would feel the earthquake from that woman's bedroom days later, sometime around noon. Pictures fell from her wall, and food fell from her cabinets. For some reason I looked for my socks while she went to the baby.

TOMBSTONE

It's 9:00 a.m. and I'm at a bar called *Doc Holiday's*. The guy who plays Doc Holiday four times a day in the reenactment down at the O.K. Corral sits a few stools down from me. I've been here a week and haven't seen him break character yet. The way the whiskey glass weighs down his disease-thin wrist makes me believe for every second he's tubercular.

I usually don't remember nights like last night, but when I woke up and saw blood all over the bathroom and carpet and those stupid little grooming scissors, I couldn't help but recall her leg looking like it was attacked by a shark, and our stupid attempt hitchhiking to the nearest hospital in Bisbee. Then I felt that stupid Super Glue all over my fingers, and I needed a drink. We could figure out this hospital business later. I kissed her and left my mouth pressed to her warm and beautiful forehead for a moment. Her hair was wild. She smelled like vanilla and like hamburgers. I let her sleep.

I had to kill a little time waiting for any of the ten bars in this town of a thousand people to open. I walked down Fremont Street, over the spot where the famous gunfight actually happened, a street, not a corral, now paved through by a state highway. You don't have to be here long to realize things about history, how it writes who's good and bad.

The bar has those saloon-type swinging doors. In walks a balding, doughy father and his son, eight or ten years old, wearing a vest with a plastic badge and a cowboy hat. The dad orders a couple glass bottles of Coke and then the kid shouts, "Doc Holiday."

Doc reaches toward his hip, places his hand on his pearl-gripped pistol, looks the father and son up and down.

The father winks to no one in particular, and then says, "He didn't mean nothing by it, Doc. He was just saying, hi." Then he pats his kid on the shoulder in a father-like way.

"I was only saying hi, too," Doc says, and holds his stare at the father and son, holds it till they get their Cokes and leave.

I watch them leave through those saloon doors too, watch the way the father exits smiling, knowing he can't wait to tell someone about this. Outside in front of the bar the guy who owns the hotel we are staying at waits with a horse and carriage for tourists. A toothless woman who was puking in the men's room of this same bar last night walks by with a pit bull, holding the leash in both hands. It's April, but believe it, snow begins to fall. The bar starts to fill. Steve, the musician from Chicago, and Ron, the retired anthropology professor from California, claim the stools between me and Doc. I have no idea yet how my life is going to change.

The author would like to thank Susan Lewis, Josip Novakovich, Richard Chiappone, David Stevenson, Jordan Herrmann, Jo-Ann Mapson and Jonathan Penton for their sound editorial advice while assembling this collection.

Some of the stories in *Highway One, Antarctica* have previously appeared in literary journals, as follows:

"Doreen and the Pig," *Cutbank*
"Polar Plunge," *The Fourth River*
"Crayon Way Outside the Lines," *Natural Bridge*
"How Dolly Parton Ruined My Life," *Tattoo Highway*
"A Terrible Sound" as "The Saddest Place on Earth," *River Styx*
"Blue Star," *River Styx*
"Sideshow," *Watershed Review*
"Highway One, Antarctica" as "The North Pole and The South Pole," *Philly Flash Inferno*
"Lighthouse" as "The Brothel War," LemonHound (Canada)
"My Last Name is Hitler," *Green Mountains Review*
"Tombstone," *Southern Indiana Review*

Justin Herrmann spent 24 months doing janitorial work at McMurdo Station in Antarctica. He lives in Alaska with his partner and daughter.

CPSIA information can be obtained at www.ICGtesting.com
Printed in the USA
BVOW05s0207080615

403626BV00003B/89/P